STAR TREK® III

SHORT STORIES

STAR TREK® III

SHORT STORIES

William Rotsler

ℛℛ

RAVETTE LIMITED
LONDON

Designed by Stanley S. Drate/Folio Graphics Co., Inc.

    Summary: Five stories featuring Captain Kirk, Spock,
and other characters from the Star Trek III movie.
    1. Science fiction, American. [1. Science fiction]
I. Title. II. Title: Star trek 3 short stories.
III. Title: Star trek three short stories.
PZ7.R753Stab 1984   [Fic]   84-2332
ISBN 0 906710 59-6

For
RON ELLIK,
absent friend

Contents

The Azphari Enigma

"**W**arp One, Mister Sulu. Set course to Earth."

"Aye aye, sir," the young officer said to Captain Kirk.

All about them repairs were being made to the damaged control room, the heart of the huge starship. In the sick bay the overworked medical personnel had the worst wounded in surgery, and in all the corridors lay others, waiting in pain for their turn.

The *Enterprise* was a badly wounded ship. In the desperate battle with Khan Noonian Singh, the Federation starship had been severely, almost mortally damaged. Warp One—the speed of light—was as much as Kirk thought the hardy old ship could take.

With the death of Captain Spock, Admiral James T. Kirk had taken just about all he could. Even the victory over Khan had not lessened his feeling of loss, of shock and anger. Only Kirk's iron discipline kept him at his tasks of getting the injured vessel and its crew back to Earth. He checked often with Commander Montgomery Scott, and had gotten the impression from the tough Scotsman that perhaps he was interfering.

"Repairs are proceeding as quickly as can be expected, sir," Scott growled over the ship's intercom. "There's only so much we can do, sir. There's structural damage, y'know. That'll take the yards back at Terra, Admiral. 'Tis more than we can do out here, sir."

"Yes, I know. Do your best, Scotty," Kirk said impatiently.

"Aye, sir," Scott said.

"Kirk out." The ship's commander fidgeted impatiently in his chair, an ache in his heart that he knew would never be eased.

Spock was dead.

Buried in space. Sent off toward the amazing new planet called Genesis. A noble death, but still . . . death. Kirk felt as if his right arm had been lost.

No, it's worse, he thought. *They could give me an artificial limb, but there is no replacement for Spock.* Kirk looked toward the Science Station, where the young Vulcan officer Saavik was at work.

She was good, but she was no Spock, and Kirk almost hated her for being there instead of the tall, taciturn Spock.

"Mister Sulu," he barked, "take the conn." Kirk heaved himself out of the command chair and strode toward the turbolift hatch. Sulu moved into the captain's chair and another lieutenant moved into Sulu's helmsman spot.

"I'm going to my cabin to clean up," Kirk said, pausing at the door to give a last scan to the control room. "Call me if there are any problems, any at all."

"Aye, sir," the Oriental officer responded. But Kirk still didn't go, reluctant to leave the nerve center of his great love.

Kirk looked at the big screen across the front of the control room. *Stars. Millions upon millions of stars. They are the final frontier . . . except for death.* Abruptly, he turned, entered the turbolift, and gave his destination as the red doors hissed closed behind him. *Worlds without number. Inhabited worlds, dead balls of rock, planets where great civilizations had risen and fallen. Planets where strange life forms had evolved from single-celled organisms into entities of great power. And new worlds, fresh and untouched, like Genesis . . . a fitting memorial to a great man.*

The lift door hissed aside and Kirk strode out into the clamor and mess of the medical deck. A young Terran technician, wounded himself, was bending over an Andorian whose legs had been badly burned by Khan's blasts. Beyond, a female Rigellian was spraying anesthetic on the burns of a cadet, who was trying desperately not to cry out.

So young, Kirk thought. *Practically children. Cadets, trainees, crew on their first spaceflight in a Federation ship.* As Kirk watched, a blood-splattered nurse pressed a hydrospray against the side of an engineer who seemed dead and the drug mixture hissed into his bloodstream. At once the Feinberger began to register life signs. The nurse flashed Kirk a smile of comradeship and directed healthy crewmen to pick the engineer up and take him to the operating room.

Was I right to take these youngsters into combat, Kirk wondered. But he knew the answer: he had had no choice. Someone had to stop Khan, and the *Enterprise* had been there.

As Kirk walked through the wounded, he knew that

the forces of what could only be called evil had to be met with the forces of good. If the good people did not resist, the bad people would prevail. The weak and helpless would die or be enslaved. Tyranny would have won. *But these brave people had fought, and fought hard,* Kirk thought. *They hadn't said, "But we aren't ready yet, come back when we are."*

Kirk was proud of them. Spock would have been proud of them. Angrily, Kirk stepped into the alcove outside the operating theater and looked in. McCoy and the other doctors were at work, patching, fixing, saving. Kirk raised a hand to the communicom by the window, then stopped. McCoy was doing his best. He always did. They didn't need a ship's captain asking if he could help. McCoy was the best and he worked hard to stay the best.

Admiral Kirk went back to the turbolift and continued on to his quarters. He stripped off the soiled and torn uniform and took a quick sonic shower, sluicing off every speck of dirt and sweat. He dressed in a new uniform and caught his reflection in a mirror.

Some commander, he thought. *Got your best officer killed. Your best friend killed.* The ache grew larger, and Kirk's face reflected his inner agony. *What could I have done differently? How could I have saved him? Khan was a mighty and deadly opponent. We barely escaped with our lives, and Spock gave his so that the rest might live.* " 'The needs of the many outweigh the needs of the few. Or the one,' " Kirk said aloud, in a harsh whisper, quoting Spock as he lay dying.

Kirk's image blurred as the tears came.

■ ■ ■

Kirk awoke at the buzz of the intercom. He glanced at the clock as he reached for the call button. An hour, he had been asleep an hour. *I've been derelict,* he thought, even though he knew he was not made of steel. Sleep was necessary. He was, in a sense, property of the Federation and should not overextend himself, for it would impair his function as a captain.

"Kirk here!"

"Admiral, we've got real trouble," Scotty said in his thick burr. "The ship—she's coming apart!"

"Where are you?" Kirk snapped as he jumped to his feet.

"Port pod support base, sir."

"Coming, Scotty!"

■ ■ ■

Kirk looked at the damage as he trotted up to Commander Scott. "Report!"

"Khan's beam cut deep, sir. Ye can see severe damage to the whole support structure there. Now, as long as we keep going at Warp One, we're all right. The stresses are equalized. But at the other end, sir . . . well, if we try to drop into impulse power, she'll tear herself apart."

"But we must stop sometime, Scotty!"

"Aye, sir, and it had better be right now. She might still be able to take it. But by the time we get to Earth—and that's the nearest shipyard—the stresses will have built up." The Scotsman shrugged. "This gallant lady will just tear herself to pieces, Admiral."

"All right," Kirk said. "We'll stop and you can make emergency repairs."

"Aye, sir, but they'll be cosmetic, practically. Enough to hold her, though."

Kirk thumbed an intercom. "Kirk here. Mister Sulu, prepare to bring the ship out of warp speed. Do it gently and slowly."

"Aye, sir," Sulu responded.

At once there was a change. The constant thrum of the great space vessel shifted. The steady thrumming sound became a growl. There was the grind and sharp ping of metal under stress. Scott yelled orders, evacuating the pod support area, and Kirk followed him out. Some of the lights shook loose under a new, sharp vibration, and an overloaded circuit snapped off.

Then there was silence.

Only the lesser, quieter throb of the ship's impulse engines filled the air. Scott let his breath out and he patted a bulkhead. "Ye did it, ye lovely thing. Ye took it." He smiled. He looked at Kirk. "I'll start on repairs at once, sir."

"Estimate of time, Mister Scott."

"Twenty to thirty hours, Admiral. Minimum. Maybe more after we get in there."

"So we're dead in the water," Kirk said uneasily. He liked maneuvering speed and maneuvering space.

"There's the impulse engines," Scotty said with injured pride. "We're not exactly a derelict, Admiral Kirk."

"No, but if a Klingon wanders by . . ." Kirk left the rest unsaid and returned to the control room.

"Status report!" he said, taking his chair from Sulu.

"On course toward Earth, sir, on impulse power. All decks report repairs underway. Doctor McCoy reports all serious patients are out of danger. And there's a star system ahead, two points southwest."

"Can you put it on the screen?" Kirk asked Saavik.

"Yes, sir, at extreme magnification."

Eight planets. One Jupiter-like gas giant. A G-type star. "Log it," Kirk ordered Saavik, who bent over her screens. Kirk watched her almost surreptitiously. She seemed unaffected by the recent battle and the death of her fellow Vulcan.

But that's how Vulcans are, Kirk reminded himself. There was nothing Saavik could do . . . except her job, and that was what she was doing. Kirk began to lose his irrational anger toward her, and to feel some guilt.

"Lieutenant Saavik, when you have finished, call your replacement and take some rest. Uhura, you, too. Mister Sulu, Chekov, Collins, Bradley, you as well."

"I'm all right, Admiral," Saavik said.

"That's an order, Mister Saavik." He softened his command with a smile. "If you intend someday to command, Mister, you must learn to take orders as well as give them."

"Yes, sir," she said unemotionally. In moments the new star system had been logged, checked through the computer, and verified as a new discovery, and Saavik turned toward her captain. "Would you like to name it, Captain Kirk?"

Kirk started to speak, then closed his mouth. Spock would have thought it an example of emotional human reaction to have a star system named after him. Besides, it might be inhabited and the natives have their own name. "No, just log it and let the computer label it."

"Yes, sir."

Twenty minutes later a new and relatively fresh crew had replaced the bridge personnel. Except for Kirk. He sat, isolated by rank and mood from the others, staring at the screen, seeing the new system draw closer.

That's why I'm here, he thought. *To go where no man has gone before. I was born to be a starship commander. To see new worlds. To seek out new life forms, new civilizations, new vistas.*

A starship captain was part scientist, part explorer, part military man. He had to be both curious and brave, cautious and bold. Kirk knew he was good, but more often than not he saw only his flaws and seldom his virtues. He was never, in his mind, quite good *enough*.

If he had been *good*, Spock would not be dead.

The intercom buzzed and Kirk slapped the control button. "Kirk here!"

"Admiral, we're gonna hafta shut down the impulse engines as well," Scotty said. "It's the vibrations, sir; we need some time at a real stillness to let the molecular welding really work."

Kirk was looking at the star system ahead. "Helmsman, how long until we can reach an orbit around that second planet?"

The helmsman punched swiftly at his board. "Two hours, four minutes, sir."

"Scotty, we'll shut down in two hours. Orbit this new planet up ahead. While you're putting the *Enterprise* back together, I'll go do something to earn my pay."

"Aye, Admiral. Two hours."

"Kirk out."

Yes, go explore a new world. Do something—anything—to avoid thinking about Spock.

■ ■ ■

"Life forms detected, Admiral," Saavik said from her post.

"Try the hailing frequency, Commander," Kirk told Uhura.

"Nothing, sir. I'll try other bands. Sir! There's something on . . . I can't make it out. Plugging into computer, Captain."

Kirk watched the magnified picture of the planet roll across the screen as they orbited the new world. It was quite Earth-like in many ways, but with a gravity of 1.3 and an atmospheric pressure at sea level of eighteen pounds per square inch. You'd feel a lot heavier there, Kirk knew, and the breathing would be harder, but it was well within tolerance levels.

"Launch probe," he ordered.

A robot dropped from the ship and raced into the atmosphere, reporting back its every find. Onboard analyzers sampled the air, digested its components, took a look at the floating spores, at the dust and microorganisms. As the probe dropped lower, it pinpointed the largest concentrations of life energy, analyzed this grouping as grazing animals, that as a higher form, and so on. Between the ship's detectors and the probe's close-in facilities, the experts on the *Enterprise* soon had a detailed picture of the planet. By that time the computer had pieced together what signals Uhura had picked up on a low-register band and reported that there was a life form that used language.

Intrigued, Kirk ordered a security team to stand by. He thumbed the intercom. "Doctor McCoy, how would you like a little shore leave?"

"Jim, I just can't. I've got an ensign here with a lung infection. There's a marine sergeant here we have to fit with a new arm, and—"

"Doctor McCoy, in your estimation, do you have an adequate surgical team?"

"Adequate! Captain . . . Admiral Kirk, they are the best! I—"

"Then you can leave things in their hands for a few hours, can't you? A little time breathing real air will do you good, and I need a medical person. Report to Transporter Room Two in fifteen minutes. Bring all your electronic black bag; and a sidearm."

"Jim, I—"

"That's an order, Doctor. Kirk out." And he grinned. It was faint and it hurt a little, but it was a grin, nevertheless.

■ ■ ■

Doctor McCoy came angrily into the transporter room. "Captain Kirk, as Medical Officer on this ship—"

"You will be needed on shore, Commander McCoy." Kirk grinned. His none-too-gentle reminder of rank made McCoy stop.

"What is this place?" he growled.

"Just another brand-new, untouched, unknown planet, Doctor. Never seen before by the beady little eyes of man."

McCoy glowered at him in a silent rebuke. "You seem in good spirits, Jim."

Kirk looked over at him, his face becoming sober. "I'm doing my job, Doctor, as I'm certain you will do yours . . . and as Spock would have done his." McCoy took a deep breath, nodded, and stepped onto the transporter disk.

The others were in place, and Kirk snapped the order to energize. The figures sparkled as the demoleculization began, and then they were gone.

■ ■ ■

"Computer link," Kirk said, glancing around him at the new landscape. It was stark, sharp-angled rocks and spiky shrubs. He felt heavy and sluggish, his breathing labored.

"Computer ready."

"Repeat any native words that might be spoken," Kirk said.

"Computer ready."

"This way. Scouts out," Kirk said. The red-clad security men sprang ahead, guns in their clips but ready to hand. "Sir!" one of them said at the crest of the rise.

Kirk clambered up next to him and looked into a valley. It was a long trough, with a purple river winding through, and what appeared to be farmlands on both sides. There were a number of buildings here and there, bell-shaped or like the minarets of Arabia. The greatest concentration was at one end of the valley, not far from them.

The minarets were cream and rose and tan in color, with needlelike tops, often ornamented with golden balls, crimson tetrahedons, and sapphire cones. The streets were curving, made of smooth gray stone, and edged with low plants in green and blue, some of which bore flowers of intense yellow.

"Are they human?" McCoy asked, squinting.

"Look for yourself," Kirk said, handing McCoy the enlarging scanner.

McCoy saw tall, graceful figures with bronzed skin, wearing simple, graceful robes. Some had jewelry, but most did not. Their heads were either shaven, or little hair grew, except for long plumes of black tendrils, coming from the crown of the skull.

"It . . . it looks Utopian," McCoy said.

Kirk nodded. "I agree. Which is exactly why I'm going to be very, very careful."

"Jim," McCoy said, "they might be timid creatures. First contact and all. Why don't we figure out some way to break it easy to them that people from—"

There was a scream, and the two men whirled to see a lean brown animal with long talons rip at the back of a screaming security man. There was a lancing blast from the phaser of a nearby crewman, and the creature tumbled to the ground.

McCoy beat Kirk to the wounded guard. The doctor's Feinberger swept over him, its lights twinkling. "Jim, we've got to get him up to the ship at once!"

Kirk dug out his communicator and flipped it open. "*Enterprise*, this is Kirk. Prepare to beam up an injured man. Alert medical. On these coordinates—"

"Stop."

They turned, and phasers were in the hands of all as they looked at the figure on the rise of rock. Kirk immediately thought of the newcomer as a she, although he had no idea why. Perhaps it was the grace, or . . . something.

"Jim!" McCoy snapped. "Order him up."

"Stop," the voice said, and Kirk realized it came not from the tall, thin figure but from the computer link, which was analyzing her words.

"This man needs attention!" McCoy snapped.

"I will heal."

Disregarding the weapons of the security team, the white-clad intruder walked down to the injured man. McCoy started to protest, and the native looked at him. There was a moment of silence as the Terran doctor looked into the large, dark, shining eyes of the new-comer. Then, without a word, he stepped back, and the female knelt by the side of the blood-spattered and torn body.

Her hands went out, and when she touched the injured man her breath sucked in in a loud hiss, as though she had touched fire. Her whole body went stiff, as though electricity was coursing through the slender limbs. The injured man stirred and moaned, his mouth sagging open in a soundless cry.

McCoy gasped as he looked at the ragged tears inflicted upon the back of the dying man. Where talons had ripped through muscle, the flesh was closing, healing even as he watched. The hiss of pained breathing was the only sound for a long moment, until one of the security men uttered an ancient Andorian oath of amazement.

"He's . . . he's closed up!"

"Look at that," another said. "It's . . . it's a miracle!"

"How do you do that?" McCoy asked as the female

lifted her hands from the torso of the man. Her liquid dark eyes seemed vacant, but the man before her breathed easily, as though sleeping, with only pink, fading scars where moments before there had been the ugly, raw, red gashes of ripped flesh.

"How do you do that?" McCoy demanded, touching the female. At once he drew back his hand, yelping in surprise. He held his hand as though it had been burnt, and demanded yet again, "You've got to tell me: *how do you do that?*"

The female sighed and slowly, gracefully, sank to the earth and seemed to sleep. McCoy blinked at her. He flipped out his communicator. "Transporter room, beam in on these coordinates. Take up the casualty. I want a complete test, and I mean from molecular tissue to brain scan! Sims, Finkelstein, go with him."

McCoy turned to Kirk. "Jim, I've got to find out what went on here!"

"Bones—"

"Jim, please. Give me time. This is fantastic, what she did!"

"All right, Doctor McCoy, you have twenty-four hours. By then Scotty will have done the repairs." His eyes narrowed on the agitated medical officer. "What about the injured on the ship?"

McCoy grabbed at Kirk's sleeve. "Jim, if I can find out how she does this; if—Jim, this could be a breakthrough like no other! No technology! A doctor could heal anywhere, anytime! Maybe we can learn to heal ourselves! Give me the time, Jim!"

"Twenty-four hours. One Earth day."

McCoy nodded his thanks and turned quickly to the

supine female. Gingerly, he touched her skin, but this time there was no sharp, tingling discharge. McCoy moved his glittering Feinberger over the length of her body, watching the readouts closely.

"She's better now. Resting, I think." He stood and looked at the city. "Is she a special person, or can they all do it? Jim, we've got to go into that city."

"I already intended to, Doctor." Kirk ordered the transporter room to beam down a life-support stretcher with two more medics.

In a few minutes the once-wounded man had been sent up, a medical team had the slender alien onto the life-support stretcher, and they were all going down the slope toward the city in the valley.

■ ■ ■

As they drew closer, they were seen, and several of the natives ran into the minarets. But most stopped and looked, surprised but seemingly unafraid. Kirk held up his hands in what he hoped was a sign of peace; at least, it was a widespread signal of peace through many races.

They walked along the dirt paths and onto the paved streets. The native on the stretcher stirred and sat up. McCoy ordered a halt and helped the slender person to her feet.

"I am Leonard McCoy. I am a doctor . . . a healer. We are all from Earth. We are members of a federation of planets. Who are you? What do you call your world?"

The limpid eyes went to the speaker of the computer link, then to McCoy's mouth, and she tilted her head for a moment, studying him, before she spoke.

"I am Saffar, Number One Medical Person of Azphar."

A graceful six-fingered hand indicated the rounded buildings of the small city.

McCoy grinned broadly. "You did something miraculous back there. That boy was all but dead! You saved his life!"

Saffar tilted her head again. "I did only my duty."

"And that's what I want to find out about," McCoy said quickly. "*How* do you do it? Is it telepathy? Some kind of body chemistry? Sympathetic medicine? What?"

A slight frown appeared on Saffar's smoothly featured face. "I do not understand. I do as we all do and have always done. It is painful, but necessary."

"You can all do it, then?" McCoy inquired with a desperate eagerness.

Again, the frown. "All? No. That would be illogical."

There was a pained expression on Kirk's face as he turned abruptly away. Logic and illogic, the poles of Spock's philosophy. Kirk watched the others like Saffar as the interrogation continued. The natives were shy, but not afraid, and in ones and twos they came out of the buildings to look at the strangers from the stars.

"Only some of you have this power, then?" McCoy asked.

"Some, yes. We all have power, as you call it. Why does your device speak our language and you do not?"

"It's an automatic translator. A simple technology. Tell me more of the powers of your people."

Saffar made a gesture to indicate those of her race around them. "Sasquin has the power to talk to the plants, to guide their growth and productivity. Almost everyone in his family has had it. It is what they do. His sister, Samari, however, does not. She is more like the Samoon family, who guide the creatures of the air."

"Is this telepathy?"

"I do not understand. We think of what we want. Sometimes it is not difficult and sometimes it is. Sometimes the changes are slow, and take generations. The great *kamali* trees, for example. Twice each day, all the members of the Surathemos family think of greater harvests from greater trees, and the trees listen, but they change very slowly, for they are as old as our culture."

"But that healing," McCoy said quickly. "You did it in moments. The flesh healed, right before our eyes!"

Again the frown. "Yes, naturally. It took longer because the structure of the flesh was different. I had to ask it how it was and it told me and I gave it the power to reform itself, to be a truly functioning part of the whole."

McCoy stared at her. "Just like that?"

Saffar tilted her head again, her smooth features unreadable. "Naturally. How else would you do it? Do you do it without the pain?"

McCoy stared at her a moment, then turned to Kirk. "Admiral, I formally request leave of absence to stay here and—"

"No, Bones," Kirk said, turning around. "You'll go back with us and finish the mission. I need you. Afterwards, afterwards if you can persuade Starfleet, you can come back."

"Jim . . ." But Kirk's expression and McCoy's years of experience with his captain told him it was no use. "All right. I have twenty-four hours."

McCoy asked to be taken to the home of Saffar, and a

delegation of natives approached Kirk. The admiral ordered another computer link beamed down; the twinkling appearance of the device caused consternation among them, then curiosity.

McCoy took one link and went off, while Kirk kept himself busy with finding out about the planet. They called it Azphari, or Earth. This did not startle or surprise Kirk. As humans explored the universe they found that most races who developed on a planet called it the Land, the Great Earth, the Place, or some similar basic word. All races evolved thinking theirs was the only world, the only self-awareness.

There were few of them. Their birthrate was low, but they lived a long time, surprisingly sturdy against a gravity that was a third heavier than Kirk's Earth. He discovered that there were families who "talked" to insects, to the larger animals, and to the drab but necessary fungi that was the ingredient of decomposition.

The lovely minarets, he found out, were the products of the Saam, a family of Azphari who talked to an almost microscopic corallike organism, directing them to crawl into the assigned places, link with those around them, and die there.

Kirk was taken to the largest minaret, where he saw beautiful and complex geometric designs edging the doorways as though carved, and, inside, intricate sculptures by the leading artists of the Saam family over the centuries.

Kirk met Sumarador, the elderly queen of Azphari, and found her eager to learn of the races beyond the lights in the sky. But Kirk's mind kept wandering. How were the repairs going? Were the injured cared for? And—always—the ache of loss for a companion.

After a time, Kirk excused himself and flipped open his communicator to call Scotty.

"It's coming, Admiral, but it's not easy. We discovered the F-21 circuit was about to blow. The matter-antimatter pod control was on the edge of fusing as well, sir. We would have had an explosion you could have seen on Pluto if we had tried to stop in Earth orbit."

"All right, Scotty, keep at it. Bridge!"

"Aye, Captain," Chekov responded.

"Chekov, give me hourly reports on the ship status. I . . . I think I'll stay here for a while."

"Aye aye, Captain."

Here, Kirk thought. *A new world. Not the familiar environment of the bridge, where a slight turning of the head would show me that Spock was not at his station. Or never would be.*

"Kirk out."

■ ■ ■

"It's time, Bones."

"Jim, there's so much to learn!"

"Doctor McCoy, Scotty says that we'll be ready to go in two hours. I want everyone on board and—"

Beep.

Kirk pulled out his communicator and flipped it open. "Kirk here."

"Captain," Chekov said, "Commander Scott reports that he's found a lot of metal fatigue in the port support main stem. It'll be another twenty hours while he shores it up."

Kirk looked annoyed and irritated. "Very well. Kirk out." He looked at McCoy. "You have another twenty hours, Doctor."

"I'll take what I can get. Jim, you just won't believe what they can do! Alter a fetus in the womb—better genetic manipulation than *we* can, and look at them! They look like they are barely out of the hunter-and-gatherer stage of civilization."

"Yes, Doctor, but my ship needs healing, too." Kirk turned and stalked away, down the paved street to the edge of the small city.

He stood and looked at the fields. The whole place was beginning to bore him. The Azphari seemed a simple race; they had art and music, but the level of complexity and sophistication was low. They could manipulate single-cell organisms to create homes, but they were basically all alike, with only minor variations. They all looked alike, as well, especially to an outsider. Their clothes *were* almost identical. They had simple mathematics and virtually no technology. They had no real natural enemies and were not warlike. They seemed like simple, good folk, but not very *interesting* people, and Kirk was keyed to a higher form of challenge. He was getting restless.

He walked back into the city, nodding pleasantly at the passing Azphari. The security men were sitting in the shade of a minaret, and he motioned them to stay sitting as he passed. He found McCoy in Saffar's domed home and motioned him outside.

"Jim, she was just telling me how they can get plants to produce certain vaccines that—"

"Bones, can they change metal?"

"I don't know, Jim. This is a very low-metal planet, you know. You'll have noticed they have almost nothing in the way of knives or tools that isn't made of wood. Why?"

"Bones, you're learning from them, right?"

"My lord, yes." McCoy beamed widely. "I don't know *how* they do it yet, but I'm finding out the range is *immense!*"

"Are they learning from you?" Kirk demanded.

"Well, I suppose so. Saffar—and the others, too, because she brought in all her family of healers—seems fascinated by physical technology. I will describe something, an operation or technique, and I'll use the computer link to show samples, and then I ask how they would do it."

"So you are learning from each other?"

"Yes, I suppose you could say that, but they're learning standard medical practice and I'm learning about something new and wonderful!"

"And they know you have a deadline?"

"I guess I mentioned it, yes."

"Doctor, is it possible they might have . . ." Kirk hesitated. The idea sounded so bizarre. But bizarreness was in the belief of the beholder. He had seen too many strange sights and had felt the effects of too many "impossible" situations to completely deny any possibility. "Is it possible they might have somehow caused the metal fatigue in the port support?"

McCoy shook his head vigorously. "No, impossible. As you know, I took Saffar and two of the others up to the ship. We were aboard three hours and they were with me the entire time. We didn't go *near* the support. I showed them the sick bay and demonstrated how the data bank worked, but they *couldn't* have done anything."

"How close to they have to be? Do they have to *touch* the object?"

"Oh, no. Close, perhaps; I'm not sure. The builders just sit out in the front, as it were, while those corallike creatures are building a dome. It's some form of telepathy, I know, but I haven't found out what. That's why I took them up to the *Enterprise*, really. To see if the sensors could read them." He shrugged. "The results were inconclusive."

Kirk nodded. "All right. But remember, you only have five hours."

McCoy nodded and trotted back to Saffar and the others, and went into an immediate huddle.

Beep.

"Kirk here!"

"Admiral, there's something funny going on here," Scott said. "I can't explain it. I inspected those structural beams myself, on the first inspection. I don't *think* I could have missed it."

"Missed *what*, Scotty?"

"The fractures. They are all through the main support, higher up than the first. But I could *swear* nothing was there before!"

"What *kind* of damage?"

"Molecular misalignment. I know it's beryllinium, but any metal can fatigue, sir, given the right circumstances. Like a few moments of a microphaser set on disruption."

"Sabotage?" Kirk asked harshly.

"No, Admiral, I don't think so. Who would be so

insane? It's either . . . well, it's natural flaws resulting from severe stresses . . . or . . . or, a disrupting beam of some sort."

"So it could be sabotage?"

There was a short silence. "I dinna like to think that, sir, but . . . it *could* be."

"When did you notice these fractures?"

"About two hours ago, Admiral. But when I looked at them when we first started orbiting this—what do you call it?"

"Azphari."

"Azphari; well, they weren't there then."

"Scotty, put on more security. Keep everyone away that isn't supposed to be there. Go to Stage Two alert."

"Aye, Admiral, but there's one other thing."

"Say it, Scotty!"

"It's Doctor McCoy, sir."

"What about McCoy?"

"Well, sir, he . . ."

"Scotty!"

"Aye, sir. Doctor McCoy and that bunch of aliens he was showing around; they were around here about the time these new flaws started."

"Bones told me he was nowhere near there."

"Well, Admiral, Ensigns Strother-Vien and Ogawa, they swear it."

Kirk's face was carefully neutral. "All right, Mister Scott, I'll look into it. Kirk out."

Captain Kirk put away his communicator looking very thoughtful.

■ ■ ■

"Jim, I tell you I was nowhere near the support, either of them!"

"There are witnesses who say so, Bones."

"Admiral Kirk, are you accusing me of *sabotage*?"

"I'm investigating, Bones. I know you want to stay here, study all this, and—"

"Jim, I wouldn't *sabotage* the *Enterprise*!" Dr. McCoy seemed genuinely amazed. "And the Azphari—you think these gentle people would wreck the ship? Jim—"

"Doctor McCoy, the Federation has never had contact with these people before. We have no idea what they would or wouldn't do. Or are capable of doing."

"But, Jim—"

"Bones, we've seen a lot of different races, different intelligent beings, from self-aware energy clouds to tele-kinetics, reptilian intelligences, remnants of ancient gods . . . Can you say for *certain* what the Azphari can or can't do?"

"No, I can't, but—"

"Then until further notice you keep the Azphari *off* the *Enterprise*. I'm getting the ship back to Earth as soon as I can. Then, Doctor McCoy, *then* you can return here and learn all you want."

"Great balls of fire, Jim! Don't you realize what a medical miracle they do here, *routinely*? I *have* to stay here, to learn—"

"*Have* to, Bones? Enough to sabotage the *Enterprise*?" McCoy's mouth snapped closed and he glared at his commander, then strode away.

Kirk pulled out his communicator. "Kirk to *Enterprise*."

"*Enterprise* here, sir," Uhura answered.

"Until further notice, neither Doctor McCoy nor any of the natives of this planet are to go aboard the *Enterprise* for any purpose."

"Doctor *McCoy*, sir?"

"Affirmative. Kirk out."

Admiral James T. Kirk turned and walked briskly toward the dwelling that had been given to his security staff as a command post. He did not notice the tall, graceful figure of Saffar step from behind a concealing decorative fungus and stare at his back.

■ ■ ■

"*Enterprise* to Admiral Kirk." Kirk pulled out his communicator, flipped it open, and identified himself. "Admiral, Commander Scott reports further damage to the port pod support."

Kirk's head went up and his face grew grim. "Uhura, order all the shields up. Complete unity. No transport window, no radio communication."

"But, sir, how will we talk to you?"

"Use the shuttles and messengers. But seal it up tight! Nothing—*nothing*—gets through!"

"Aye, sir. *Enterprise* out."

Kirk looked at the now useless communicator in his hand, then put it away out of habit. He looked at the handful of security men in the corallike structure. Four. Tough, intelligent, the Marines of the space fleet. But only four.

"Sergeant Gregg, yellow alert."

"Aye, sir!" Gregg turned at once and checked the status of each of his team of three. Then they followed Kirk to the minaret-house of the family of Saffar. He strode through the curtained opening, and found Leonard Mc-Coy bent over a table, staring at a small furry animal with protruding teeth and long claws.

"Bones!"

"Jim! Oh, you've got to see this! Quick! See that pink line, see? It's fading. A minute or so ago it was severed! The whole limb removed! Now look at it: healing! Jim, this is the most amazing—"

"Bones!" Kirk pulled McCoy back, his eyes staring fiercely at the half-dozen tall Azphari surrounding the table. "Doctor! These people have somehow blinded you! They've sabotaged the *Enterprise*! They want to keep us here!"

"Aw, Jim, be reasonable. We can learn from them. What can we teach *them*? Now, look, the fur is growing back. Isn't that amazing?"

Kirk turned to stare hard into the large, limpid eyes of Saffar. "You're doing it, aren't you? You're causing the pod support to fall apart. You're making the metal *rot*!"

"Jim, be reasonable," McCoy protested. "Metal doesn't rot, these people can't—"

"They can and they *are*! I don't know *how*, but they are. Maybe there are submicroscopic metal-eating microbes chewing away, maybe they are depolarizing the atoms, I don't know, but they *are* doing it." His eyes locked with those of Saffar. The eyes were huge, liquid, without depth.

"Man of the other Earth, we only wish to learn," Saffar said.

"No, you wish to keep us here, learn our technology, our—" Kirk stopped, his eyes bulging. His hands went to his throat and he turned red. Phasers leaped into the hands of the security men, but before they could fire they flung them aside violently, as if they were on fire. Then they, too clutched at their throats, gasping hoarsely.

"Stop it!" McCoy screamed. "Stop it!" McCoy jumped across the table, his hands going for the throat of Saffar, but she stepped back. McCoy gasped and fell unconscious. The small furry creature squirmed out from under and scampered away.

Saffar looked down at the limp figures of the six spacemen. At a gesture, the figures began breathing again, but they were still unconscious. Saffar bent down and removed Kirk's communicator. She hesitated a moment, then spoke into the communicator in a perfect imitation of Jim Kirk's voice.

"*Enterprise*, this is Kirk. Come in, please." A faint frown creased the smooth face of Azphari's Number One Medical Person. "*Enterprise*, this is Admiral James T. Kirk, come in, please."

Nothing.

Saffar growled and threw aside the communicator. With eye contact she drew together the other Azphari, and they concentrated. Sweat appeared on their smooth features, but at last they broke contact. Saffar strode angrily from the minaret, and outside there appeared, coming from every field and structure, all the Azphari adults.

They stood silently in the square before the house of the old queen, their features strained and harsh as they sought to break through the electronic screens of the *Enterprise*.

Then Saffar jerked, and the linked net dissolved. She marched stiffly back into her home and stared at the Earthmen. In a few moments they regained consciousness and sat up, rubbing aching heads and whispering through raw throats.

"They blocked our air passages," McCoy said. "Caused our own flesh to grow and—"

"Never mind, Bones, there's something more important now." Kirk got shakily to his feet. "You couldn't break through, could you?" He smiled thinly at Saffar. "Powering those screens is a power plant big enough to light a small planet. You'll never break through."

Saffar spoke, and the translator clicked. "You will get us aboard or you will die. Your own bodies will attack you. You will know pain driven to the ultimate and yet live."

"Saffar!" McCoy said in astonishment. "You're not like that, you're—"

"But she is," Kirk said. "They all are. They want to get off this planet. We've shown them the civilizations of the stars, and they want to go see. Can you imagine them out there? Who could resist? They can make our own bodies betray us."

"Exactly, Earthman Kirk," Saffar said. "And you will help us."

Kirk shook his head. "I'm afraid not, Saffar. Oh, you can hurt me, you can hurt us. But we were not selected for our mission because we were weak, nor because we did not understand the dangers. We will probably die. It will not be pleasant, I'm sure. I'm going to hate it a lot. But the alternative . . . the alternative is to let the Azphari loose on the Federation, and, after the Federation, the Romulans and the Klingons, too. As much as I'd like to see them bothered, I would not wish you upon even them."

Saffar looked at Kirk for a long moment, then, abruptly, Kirk screamed and his body bent backward in a spastic jerk that made him cry out again. "Stop it!" McCoy said. "I'll get you aboard! Stop hurting him!"

"No." Kirk's voice was weak and harsh as he grunted out his protest. "Don't."

"Jim, they're killing you!"

Kirk gasped and his muscles contracted, his skin tightened. Through the tight-fitting Starfleet uniform McCoy could see every muscle of Kirk's body clearly outlined, as if in the grip of a huge squeezing invisible hand. The Starfleet admiral croaked out another "No!" to McCoy before his head fell back as his consciousness left.

But almost at once consciousness returned as Saffar restored the blood flow. Kirk screamed in pain as his own blood seemed like acid in his veins. His skin was on fire. Everything hurt, *everything*.

"I'll tell you how!" McCoy screamed, and abruptly Kirk slumped to the ground, to lie limp and unconscious.

"How, Earthman?" Saffar asked.

McCoy hesitated, then his body jerked painfully. McCoy stared at his hands. His fingers had grown together, the skin thickening as he watched, until he had thick paddles for hands. The doctor cried out, but Saffar was merciless. "How?" she asked softly.

"My hands." Saffar nodded and the skin thinned, his fingers split apart, and in moments he was whole again.

"The shuttle. The ship will send down a shuttle."
Saffar smiled.

■ ■ ■

The shuttle dropped out of the blackness of space and angled in smoothly toward the single city. It set down just outside the cluster of minarets and Kirk, McCoy, Gregg, and the security men strode briskly toward it. The hatch came down, and they entered. Moments later, the hatch closed and the shuttle lifted.

"Well, Doctor McCoy, did you learn something on Azphari?"

"Yes, Admiral Kirk, I did. They are a harmless race, but with great medical skills. After we return to Earth, I will return here to study."

"Good, Doctor McCoy, I'm certain it will do us all good." Kirk stared out the port at the darkening sky. The shuttle cleared the last wisps of atmosphere and took an arcing orbit toward the *Enterprise*.

"Shuttlecraft *Columbus*, this is the *Enterprise*. Security check. Please respond."

"*Enterprise*, this is Admiral James Tiberius Kirk. I am coming aboard."

"Admiral Kirk, please respond with Security Clearance Sequence One."

Kirk looked at McCoy and their faces contorted with effort as their minds sought to probe through the starship's defensive screens. Their figures blurred and rippled as the effort of mind took away from their efforts to maintain their illusion as Federation officers. The security men, too, sloughed off the Terran images and reclaimed their Azphari identities.

The young lieutenant at the security post gasped and fell back, but not before he slapped the intruder alarm.

At once a nerve gas, keyed to the central nervous system of ninety-six races, billowed into the *Columbus* cabin. The Azphari fell at once, for their nervous system was within the parameters of several of those ninety-six.

■ ■ ■

The shimmering bars of light all around the Azphari village became armored security men, their battle phasers at the ready. They approached the minarets carefully. The moment they saw an Azphari, they fired, the phasers set on stun. In minutes their detectors brought them to the minaret where Kirk and his crew lay tied up.

"Well, Doctor McCoy, do you still want to stay here and study the medical technology of Azphari?" Kirk asked, rubbing his wrists.

"Yes, I do, but I won't." He sighed. "They have such wonders to teach us. They would have been welcomed with open arms." He sighed again, looking to where the *Columbus* has set down and the unconscious Saffar and her people were being offloaded. "It means they'll be off limits, doesn't it?"

"That's what I'll recommend," Kirk said. "We'll leave the standard Federation indoctrination package. And every few years they'll get checked out by people who know what to expect. Maybe someday they'll learn how to get along with other people, to respect them, respect their rights."

McCoy nodded. "I can live with that, but . . ." He sighed again. "Well, thank heavens you built in some security checks."

"They had the look, they had the words, Doctor," Kirk said, "but they just didn't have the rhythm." He flipped open his communicator. "Kirk to *Enterprise*. Beam Doctor McCoy and myself up. Tell Commander Scott I want an estimate of time on the completion of his repairs. And ask the cook to prepare something special for dinner tonight." Kirk looked at McCoy. "Doctor, have you anything special you'd like?"

"Anything that doesn't fight back," McCoy grumbled. He looked at the cluster of minarets, thinking of the scientific and medical wonders that were going to be prohibited until the race that developed them learned to live in peace with their neighbors. "Let's go, Jim," McCoy said.

Kirk looked around one final time, and couldn't help asking himself if what he had done was what Spock would have done. He lifted the communicator to his lips. "Activate," he ordered.

McCoy and Kirk shimmered and were gone. The *Columbus*, with the security men aboard, lifted into the sky. All was still for long moments, then the first of the Azphari stirred and awoke.

Saffar raised her liquid dark eyes toward the heavens, her face expressionless. A tear formed in the corner of one great eye and trickled erratically down her smooth cheek.

The
Jungles
of
Memory

Personal Log, Lieutenant Commander Nyota Uhura. Stardate 8210.1

While the *Enterprise* is undergoing repairs in space-dock, we have been given leave to go earthside. Although in terms of time it has not been long since we had been on Earth, in terms of physical and emotional stress it seems like ages. I'm taking the government shuttle down, my face pressed to a porthole, watching the most beautiful sight in the galaxy.

We've been to a lot of planets, my shipmates and I, from the stark beauty of Vulcan to the lush jungles of Leighvien, from spinning balls of war-blasted rock to great city-worlds like Rothstein II. But there has been nothing to compare to Terra. The big blue marble. The home planet. Once thought to be the center of the universe, it is still center to *homo sapiens*.

When I left, to first go into space, I didn't really want to come back. Jomo Murambi, my first love, had been killed in the service of his country, our country, the

United States of Africa. Getting out into space, getting away from things that reminded me of him—and everything did—was as important as the job I was undertaking. Then, when I was posted to the *Enterprise*, his memory began to fade. It will never disappear, never, but I have it in a safe place now, a place in my heart where not *everything* can hurt it. So I *can* go home now. Back to Earth, back to Africa, back to Nairobi, back to my family.

It's been a long time.

I think I can take it.

We're setting down at Sahara Spaceport in a few minutes. Home at last.

■ ■ ■

Personal Log, Supplementary

It's been quite a day. Sahara has grown since I was here last. It's one of the chief terminals for solar system travel. I saw ore ships from the asteroids, a bulgy science ship in from Pluto, shuttles from two of the Moon bases, a big tourist liner outward bound for Jupiter and Saturn, and lots of the little ore-catchers buzzing back and forth. They're rather cute, like bumblebees. All the rich mines on Luna pack up processed metal ore into uniform "bullets" that are electrically propelled off tracks on the Moon—mass accelerators working against the low gravity there—and they go into close Earth orbit. Then these little ships go out, snag 'em, and bring down the cargo. We have a rich system, but we only narrowly averted ecological disaster in the late twentieth century, until we learned how not to foul our own nest.

I took an Air Africa jet to Nairobi. Lake Victoria looked so beautiful as we came down over Kampala. I remembered water-skiing there as a girl, fishing, swimming, the picnics. Then we were down.

I saw Malcolm first, because he's taller, then my little sister Uaekundu. My older brother is a big, handsome man with a lovely wife and two children. I spent the day with them, getting reacquainted and making friends with my niece and nephew. They hadn't seen me since they were practically babies and didn't know me, really.

Uaekundu had left college up in Cairo to greet me and we caught up on things. But I kept looking at the children, wondering if I had missed something. I couldn't decide then, and I can't decide now, if I have.

I've done things, seen things, been places my brother and sister cannot imagine. On my first starship, the *Elst Weinstein*, as Assistant Communications Officer, I saw more in the first year than I had ever even read about in all my years of school! The galaxy is so big it is impossible to grasp! So rich in variety, so immense, so dangerous—and so exciting!

I have to keep reminding myself there are *millions* of galaxies!

Then, in my other ships—with the *Enterprise* being my heart of hearts—I saw so much more. Alien worlds, alien creatures, strange life forms, societies so different from ours that they were almost unrecognizable as societies. These people are my family, yet . . . yet the crew of the *Enterprise* is my *real* family. We have shared so much together, not only the dangers, but the comradeship, the laughter, and the realization that we were doing something really important.

I was a stranger in the bosom of my own family. I knew that and they knew that. They were like strangers; *I* was like a stranger to them. I think *they* think I think they are stuck-in-the-mud, while I go off on missions of glory. It's true, I couldn't really settle down, not now at least; but I certainly don't think they are lacking in courage or have not made the right decisions. Some people simply require different lives.

Little sister Uaekundu was just bubbling over. Her famous sister was back. "Is Khan really dead? What is that handsome Captain Kirk like? The Vulcan, Commander Spock, is he—" and so on. My autobiography, *Space, The Final Frontier*, had just been published, and I regretted having written it. Perhaps such things should be published after you're dead and gone. But after Captain Kirk became an admiral and most of us had been transferred off the *Enterprise*, it seemed as though an era had come to an end. We never guessed we'd actually ever get together again, much less have such an experience as fighting Khan.

It had been a strange time. We had been scattered, and like disciplined people and career Starfleet officers, we had done as we had been told, even James T. Kirk. Chekov had been promoted and had gone off to the *Nelson*, later to the *Reliant*. Doctor McCoy had taken duty at Starfleet Academy. Scotty had gone over to the *Yorktown*. Sulu had been promoted, too, and had been posted to the *Regulus* as Chief Helmsman. Mister Spock had gone to Starfleet Academy, too, then had taken a leave of absence. And, of course, Captain Kirk had been placed on the faculty at Starfleet Academy. I'd gone to the *Antares*, but then we'd all come flying back to be with Captain Kirk when he'd asked for us.

But before we encountered Khan on that fateful training flight, it *had* seemed a period in our lives had come to an end. I know Captain Kirk had felt that way. "The Peter Principle," he had told me once, when I visited him at the Academy. "A twentieth-century philosopher defined it perfectly. 'In a hierarchy individuals tend to rise to their level of incompetence.'"

I had disagreed, of course. There was so *much* James Kirk could teach recruits, but he had disagreed. "I'm a starship captain, not a schoolteacher. I belong out there," he said, gesturing toward the skies.

I couldn't argue with that, but I felt sad, too. At the time I *never* dared hope we'd all be together again. Starfleet just isn't that nice. Winning teams do get broken up, if there's a reason. Our reason was the end of voyage. I suppose the Powers That Be thought they were being nice to us, giving us easier duty. And it is true on some ships that tensions build, relationships undergo strain, and tempers flare.

Oh, to be sure, some of us from the old ship were still out in starships. Still out there on the line. But the "chemistry" in the *Enterprise* had been so special. We *had* gone where no man had gone before. Space *is* the final frontier.

So, sensing that was the end of an era, I succumbed to pressure and dictated my autobiography. I felt a little foolish doing it, it seemed so egotistical, but yet I did want the stories told—the ones Starfleet authorized us to tell, that is—and to tell of Kirk, Spock, and the others. I was proud, so proud, to have been a part of that team.

I wasn't the only one to write something. Many biographies and autobiographies were done, histories of space exploration were written. Some were highly colorful, and some were highly inaccurate, too! That was another reason for me to write: to set the stories down correctly.

So, toward the end of that first week back home, just before my little sister went reluctantly back to school, I appeared at one of the Dangerous Visions bookstores in Nairobi to autograph copies. Little sister Uaekundu was bursting with pride. I kept hearing her tell strangers, "That's my sister."

I have never understood autographing. I suppose it shows that the owner of the book was close enough to "greatness" or something. I don't mean to insult those people. It is flattering to be asked, to be considered important enough to be asked, but I don't really understand what having an autograph proves.

I was asked the kind of questions I often get asked—"Is it all true?" and "What is Mister Spock really like?"—but with one added question: "Who is Jomo Murambi?" I had dedicated the book to him, and now I found it very sad that a valiant officer, who had given his life for his country, was remembered by his nation only as a dedication in a book.

That's something else. For over five hundred years a "book" was a physical thing, paper pages with printing on them, then metal foil pages. Now a "book" was electrons in a microchip, and my "autograph" was electronically added on a terminal in the bookshop, printed under a moving image taken as I spoke the autograph.

In many ways these are better books, at least physically. They won't deteriorate or age. Authors can include still pictures, moving images, frozen frames, charts, maps, animation, whatever they want. I had gotten permission to reproduce crucial events recorded by the *Enterprise*'s visual log. It hadn't been easy, for Starfleet is a closed-mouth organization about some things. But I had gotten to know Lee Friedrich in the Public Information Office and he had convinced his superiors the publicity would be good for Starfleet. I had been told that recruitment did rise shortly after the "book" was released, especially among women, and most especially in the United States of Africa.

In any case, I was sitting at the terminal autographing away, and I finished with one fan and turned to take the next microchip from the next in line. I saw a man's hand, wide and strong, holding out the chip. I glanced up, and my heart stopped.

He was tall, dark, and not exactly handsome. He seemed rough-hewn, almost unfinished, yet . . . strong, and, as I was to realize later, perfect for him. He wore a plain dark shalmar jumpsuit that emphasized his broad shoulders and slim waist. I guess something showed on my face, because his smile broke across his face like a sunrise.

"Hello, Nyota," he said.

I blinked. "Uh, hello," I said politely, carefully masking my confusion. This man disturbed me greatly and I couldn't understand *why*.

"You don't remember me, do you?" he asked.

"Wait, I . . . there's something . . ." My eyes widened and my mouth dropped open as I recognized in the grown man the lean teenager of my youth. "Oh, my. Is it you, Somabula?"

His grin was my answer. Impulsively I jumped up and hugged him, then kissed him on the cheek. "Let me look at you," he said, holding me at arm's length. "A long time since that skinny little girl came to Kenya Park."

I laughed. "I was never *skinny*. Slender, perhaps."

I looked at him fondly. It had been so long before. The memories rushed back. Kenya Park was my favorite place in the galaxy. They had restored it to its nineteenth-century beauty. There were lodges, yes, but you arrived by silent ground vehicles, not by plunging out of the sky and frightening the animals. Aircraft were, indeed, forbidden to pass over at less than 85,000 feet. It had become a paradise again. The herds had been built back up, painstakingly, carefully, Poachers were dealt with severely. My own father had moved there, to take up residence in a restored *kraal* of our ancestors, to live out his retirement years in what many would consider extreme primitive conditions, which only showed their ignorance.

Somabula had been an apprentice Ranger then, a tall and somber guardian of the ecology. I had a crush on him all those summers of my youth. Year after year, when I visited there, I had always wanted to go past his station, to camp nearby. I had thought he had never noticed me, at least never noticed me until I was sixteen, anyway.

He had taken me on marking tours. Well, me and some of my schoolmates. We had implanted biological "labels" in the tusks of young elephants, to aid in tracing the ivory later should it be poached. The tracers had become a harmless part of the entire tusk, impossible to remove. Once he had allowed me to help him in fixing a broken leg on a young mammoth, one of the fifth generation cloned from the cells of the ancient creatures found in Arctic ice.

Now here he was. The years dropped away, and we were under the great trees again. The elephant herd was not far off, led by Bruce, my own name for my special elephantine friend. And there, I had gotten my first kiss. My first *real* kiss, I mean.

He had seemed so much older then, almost four years my senior, grownup and mature. We had written during that winter, then I went off to school and the visits to the Park grew less frequent and sometimes I missed him, and Jomo had come along, then Starfleet and all the rest.

"Somabula," I said.

"Uh, there are other people waiting, Commander," the bookstore owner whispered discreetly.

"Wait for me?" I asked, and Somabula nodded. I took his chip and set it aside and finished with the others. For the first time ever, I was glad there were only a few customers left. Then I spoke something into his copy and we went to lunch.

I asked about Elayne, Bruce's mate, and Baso, Limpopo, Logengula, Selous, and Gandang, the other elephants. And Boris, Ivan, and Natasha, the mammoths. I found that Mzilikazi, the Chief of the Park Rangers, had retired and Somabula was First Assistant to Jonathan Mukusi, the new Chief Ranger. With questions that were perhaps none to artful I found that Somabula had been married, fathered two sons, but that his wife had been killed in a shuttle crash on Zanzibar four years before.

"Come to the Park," he suggested, and I nodded.

"I was going up to see my father and . . ." I'm afraid I blushed. "I wonder if you might have time for me."

He just grinned. Sometimes men can be so egotistical!

■ ■ ■

Personal Log, Supplementary

There are times when I wonder why I keep a log. Habit, I suppose. All those years of log-keeping in starships. They had come in handy when I wrote my book, of course, but there are times when I think they are just too egotistical. As if people would be interested in what *I* have to say! But when I dictate, I am not really thinking about *others* ever reading this.

You know how you sometimes have to explain something to someone else? Maybe you think you know all about a subject, but when you go to actually verbalizing it, you find you have made a number of unwanted assumptions, *assumed* certain facts or ideas to be true, and generally have not actually thought it all out. *That's* why I do these log entries. To figure out my life.

I remember being interviewed by a UBC reporter when we came home from that first long trip on the *Enterprise*. The questions she asked showed what a tremendous gap there was between the reality of Starfleet and space exploration and the public perception of it. She thought there was nothing out there but terrible bug-eyed monsters, rapacious Klingons, and treacherous Romulans. That we lived shoulder to shoulder as in twentieth-century submarines, and that the discipline aboard starships was not unlike being under Captain Bligh of the H.M.S. *Bounty*.

Wrong.

In explaining to her the realities, I had looked at my own life from a different angle. I had seen how "glamorous" it looked, how dangerous and exciting. Yet I could never make her understand the *satisfaction* of teamwork and accomplishment, of meeting challenges that quite literally have never been encountered before in the history of man. I couldn't make her understand how great was my respect for my crewmates—not only Captain Kirk and Commander Spock, or McCoy, Sulu, Scott, Chekov, Doctor Chapel, but the engineers and specialists, the ordinary spacemen and women, the cadets and yeomen. Dedicated, concerned, involved—all these were words that seemed to bounce right off her.

She saw the crew of the *Enterprise* as a combination of military adventurers and pirates, as exploiters and conquerors.

"You don't *conquer* space," I had said. "You *learn* it. Nature is not something you defeat; you learn to live with it." But she had this preconceived idea, a romantic and also insulting idea, of how we were, what we did, and why we did it.

There are people who are—to use a spaceman's term—"mud-ballers." It's not that the mud-ballers are afraid—though that can be true as well—but that they are blinded. They live as they live and seek not, see not, beyond their limited vision. They are the ones that strip the forest, gut the earth, foul the seas because they cannot see, in their own lifetime, what they have done to Mother Earth. They think to seek knowledge beyond a practical application of science to technology is some kind of aberration, a sickness. To go where no man has gone before is madness to them.

People like this can never understand that each bit of knowledge we gain is a step toward understanding not only Nature, but ourselves as well, for we cannot separate ourselves from Nature. In that interview I truly realized for the first time what a different sort we of Starfleet are.

In some ways we are closer to those in the Klingon space fleet than to certain of our own race, those who have never looked at the night sky and truly *wondered*.

■ ■ ■

Personal Log, Supplemental

When I went to Kenya Park, it all came back. The vast, rolling veldt, the trees and animals, and that feeling— which I had felt only on other planets—that here the hand of man had not spoiled things. It was an illusion, of course. It was the hand of man that had, against great opposition as far back as the nineteenth century, *restored* Kenya to its "original" state, and it had taken years and donations from all over the world, and from colonies of Earth as well.

I went to the village where my father lived, and it was like stepping back in time. At the Park entrances we are given a choice of clothing to wear. One choice is a kind of elegant flowing white robe, which is timeless . . . and you are totally ignored. You don't exist. You cannot intrude. You are unseen, or so is the custom. It is the height of rudeness to wear the white robe and to force yourself on anyone.

But it is disconcerting at first. You can walk into a hut, observe a family at its most intimate and private moments, and not be "seen" at all. People will literally walk into you or over you, and pretend to have stumbled. I've tried the white robe, but I much prefer the second choice, that of the native garb of the area.

Dressed in that manner, you are not only "seen" but you are involved, whether you are black, white, or

Oriental. (Non-human races must use white robes.) You are taken as you are, for whoever you are, and greeted as a real person. "I see you, Nyota," my father said, giving me the traditional welcome. I was seen, I was acknowledged, I existed. I embraced my father.

In his hut I saw the pottery he was making. It was lovely, but bore only a token appearance to the traditional pottery of the area.

"If we freeze our culture," he said, "we become relics, cultural fossils." He gestured at the huts around the square. "This is as it was when the white man came. What I have done is acknowledge the existence of the whites, and incorporate their presence into my designs."

I thought of the old sculptures in Bali that showed men in western hats, in early automobiles, bearing weapons and tools contemporary to the times. This, I realized, is what my father had done.

"Every culture progresses, or dies," he said. "The Aztecs changed with the invasion of the Spanish, but changed in a way that almost obliterated their culture. We here are trying a second time, to not be overwhelmed by the invaders, but to accommodate them, as the Chinese did with every invading horde. They *absorbed* them and took from them what they wanted. Canada, that province of United North America when it was independent, had an enlightened policy with the Eskimos, to preserve as best they could their culture and art, untouched as much as possible by commercial greed."

I left my father after two days and took a dusty ride to where Somabula was stationed.

■ ■ ■

Personal Log, Supplemental

It's been a while since I put an entry in the log, but I've been busy. My, is *that* an understatement!

Somabula was glad to see me, and he had set up a field trip into a pretty isolated stretch of the Park. I know many people think of the Park as part veldt and part impenetrable Tarzanesque jungle, but the "jungle" part is mostly exaggerated. Still, there are places where the growth is thick and the ground shadowed from high trees reaching toward the sun.

It's Park policy to keep certain areas undisturbed, even by tourists, with only infrequent visits by Park Rangers to monitor the area. I suspect Somabula had "opened" up one of those areas just for me. So what we headed into had not been visited even by a Ranger for over a year, and not by tourists for almost ten. They want to let the animals "settle in" and be undisturbed, and I agree.

It was just Somabula and me. We took a silent ground vehicle to the perimeter of the restricted zone, then hiked in. At once I fell under the thrall of the primitive jungle. Birds, small animals, flowers, the distant roar of a lion—all combined to throw me back to my youth. In my youth such an experience always made me travel back in time to some undefined period hundreds of years before, when there was no technology more advanced than a spear. Perhaps it was an anticipation of that feeling that had made me leave behind my off-duty phaser, my communicator, everything of contemporary times. Both of us dressed in versions of eighteenth-century native clothing, and we carried only knives, and Somabula a spear.

Yes, I know, both romantic and foolish. We cannot go back and even if I could—for real, that is—I probably wouldn't. Those times are romantic, but the world was filled with ignorance, disease, slavery, death, and plague.

Neither of us was prepared for the bright blue slash of a beam that narrowly missed Somabula and brought crashing down a young tree. A limb knocked Somabula unconscious, and branches threw me into the underbrush.

I lay for a moment, stunned, not quite understanding what had happened. *A blue beam?* A phaser blast! *Someone had tried to kill us!*

I couldn't believe it. I didn't *want* to believe it. Not here, not in the paradise of my youth.

I heard a thrashing in the underbrush on the other side of a gully, on the hillside where the deadly beam had originated. I squirmed around and looked at Somabula and thought he was dead. There was blood on his head, and I couldn't see any sign of his breathing. I tried to crawl closer, but I heard the movement in the brush again. I crawled quickly into the shelter behind the great trunk of a tree and drew my knife, a poor weapon against a phaser.

I used the cover of a fern to look back toward the severed tree and saw something I thought I would *never* see on Earth! A Klingon!

There was no mistaking him. The swarthy skin, the black and maroon clothing, the dully gleaming scarf of rank, the Klingon hand weapon, the dark and deadly eyes.

I shrank back out of sight and tried to think. What was a Klingon doing here? Were there more of them? What were they up to?

As I thought, I realized no Klingon could go unreported in any of the civilized parts of Terra; but on the other hand, what could one, or even several, do in the loneliness of Kenya Park? *How* they got here was of less importance than *what*. They could have bribed or hidden aboard a freighter, then stolen away in the night to this remote spot.

But what were they planning?

My first thought was to report all of this to Captain Kirk. I cursed myself for not having retained my communicator, if for no other reason than to report any medical emergency. But no, I had to "go native" in the extreme.

First I had to survive; then, to report. I heard movement in the brush, and a grunt. I peeked out again and saw the Klingon turn over Somabula with his toe. The Klingon looked around, then pulled my friend up, tying his hands with a leather thong found in the haversack Somabula was carrying.

If he's tied, I thought, it means Somabula is alive. I watched surreptitiously as the Klingon secured Somabula's hands to a limb, then tied his feet, leaving him staked out.

A goat.

In India they used to hunt tigers by staking out a goat and watching in ambush for a hungry tiger to take the bait.

Somabula was the goat, I was evidently the tiger. The Klingon was counting on the humanity of the "native" he had seen to attempt a rescue. I sat back and thought.

"Never fight by your opponent's rules," Jim Kirk had said. "Do not let him or her choose the ground, nor the time, nor the way of battle, not if you can help it." I mentally sent a message to Somabula: *Hold on. I cannot attempt to rescue you, for I will die and the secret be lost.* It was more important that Starfleet should know that one or more Klingons were here on Earth.

I backed off and slipped into the underbrush as quietly as I could. All those games I had played as a child came back to me: Watch your shadow, watch where you put your feet, don't get boxed in, keep them guessing, move silently and swiftly, don't get predictable.

I used every bit of cover to get myself a couple of hundred yards away. Then I rose and started trotting through the jungle back toward the vehicle we had left behind.

Please, don't let the Klingon kill him, I prayed as I ran. Then suddenly a shape rose up and a fist crashed into the side of my head, and as I fell, everything blacked out.

I awoke next to Somabula, with both of us tied hand and foot. The bleeding on his head had stopped, but he was not conscious. His breathing was shallow, and I felt he was dying.

Suddenly my head was wrenched around and there was an ugly Klingon face snarling into mine. He spoke Universal, his words harsh, his breath bad.

"Speak, Earthdog! Why are you here?"

He must not know I am from Starfleet, I remember thinking. "I . . . I was just with the Ranger, the Park Ranger. I'm . . . I'm his . . . we are to be married, and I—"

The Klingon snarled and wrenched back my head. I let out a scream of terror—not all of which was faked—to convince him I was only a kind of tourist. I knew he would kill me, and Somabula, too. He could not afford to let us go, however innocent. But I hoped to lull him as he pumped me for information. Already I was trying to work loose from the leather thong that strapped my hands behind my back. I squirmed and writhed in fright to disguise my motions.

He growled other questions at me. Were there others? What were we doing there? At last he grew even more angry, and I knew my time was close. With a snarl, he shoved me back and stood up. My wrist bonds were loosened, but I was still not free.

He adjusted his phaser and I thought, *I'm going to die*. Then he turned away to a clear patch of ground and began to move the phaser back and forth over it, the blue beam disintegrating the ground.

He was making a grave.

I tore the skin on my wrists as I tugged at the thong, but a little skin was a small price to pay for a chance at life. Suddenly, my wrists were free. His back was turned, the grave taking up his concentration. I bent my legs, lying on my side, and brought my ankles up to my fingers. The knot was tied tightly and difficult to unravel, as it was a strange and overly elaborate Klingon knot.

Then my legs were free. Without a moment's hesitation, afraid of being discovered and having the disintegrating beam swing around to me, I kicked out at the Klingon. He shouted gutterally and pitched forward. The wildly waving phaser blazed through several nearby plants before he fell sprawling into the half-made grave.

I was on my feet quickly, swaying and grimacing with pain as the circulation returned. My head already throbbed badly from the blow that had felled me. I lurched toward the edge of the grave, where the phaser lay in the dirt.

But the Klingon recovered quickly and reached for it. I

knew I would not get to it in time, so I stomped on it. I caught his fingers under my heel, and he yelped. The weapon cracked, its plastic ruptured, but it might still have been functional. As the Klingon reached again, I kicked again. Pain shot up through my foot, but I heard the crunch of electronic parts and another yelp of outrage from the Klingon.

I staggered about a moment, then, as the Klingon pulled himself from the grave, I kicked him hard on the chin. The shock traveled up my leg to knock me on my back, but the Klingon fell backward into the grave and lay still.

I caught my breath and stood with chest heaving, looking at him. He was alive, and I knew that if our places were reversed, he would have killed me in an instant. But I could not. Certainly not in cold blood. I found the leather thongs I had been bound with, and untied Somabula as well, then tied up the Klingon.

I pulled Somabula to his feet. His head lolled loosely, and fresh blood appeared on the bandage I had contrived. I had to get back to the Park Station as soon as possible, not only to report the Klingon's presence, but to save the life of my friend.

I found our spear and used it as a crutch as I helped drag and carry Somabula along. I had forgotten just how heavy the dead weight of a full-grown man was. I thought about putting him into a hiding place, running back to the ground car, and getting professional help, but I was afraid the Klingon would find him. The leather thongs would not hold him forever. I had had little practice in tying up anyone, much less a burly Klingon. Sooner or later he would get loose.

Or be found by other Klingons.

As I enter this into my log, and if anyone reads it, they will know that I survived, but I must say that it didn't seem that way as I lived it. I was exhausted within a half-mile and decided I *had* to find Somabula some place to rest, then go on by myself; it was simply taking more time and therefore was more dangerous to him.

But I found nothing suitable. There were no caves, no little nooks in which to hide him. He was unconscious and perhaps would become conscious, or cry out in pain in his sleep, and be discovered. I struggled on, but my reserves of strength were diminishing quickly. I ached from fatigue and from my own, lesser, injuries. I *had* to stop.

Then I remembered something Somabula had told me long ago: hunters seldom look up. They watch the spoor upon the ground, the bush, the tracks, the land ahead, but seldom up into the trees. I began searching and soon found something: the deep crotch of a great tree.

If I could get him up there, he might be safe. I'd gag him to keep him from crying out, and if he was coherent as he awoke—unbound but gagged—he would get the idea. I hoped.

It took me forever to get him into the tree. I had to tear up most of my clothing to make straps to pull him up. Luckily my skirt was generous enough to retain some coverage, though frankly, at the time, I was not thinking as much about that as sheer survival.

I gagged him and left him in the ruins of a bird's nest and climbed down and started wearily off toward the edge of the jungle.

Suddenly, a blue beam flashed next to me, searing off

fern leaves and slashing through the bark of a nearby tree. Instantly I threw myself into the brush, rolled, bruising myself on the spear's shaft, and then, in concealment, crept in another direction.

The beam zapped again, then again and again, stabbing randomly into the underbrush, disintegrating the foliage. The pungent scent of slashed plants was in my nose as I tried to press myself into the damp earth. This was no stun beam, this was the killing beam of a deadly Klingon weapon.

I had to lead him away from Somabula, yet stay alive. I moved as silently as I could, slithering like a dark snake through the brush. I found a stone and crept on, holding it tightly in my hand.

The Klingon's beam cut randomly through the cool green underbrush; everywhere was the slithery sound of several limbs falling, as I used the noise to move unheard.

Then I heard the Klingon speak—and another answered!

There were two of them, or more. That explained why the Klingon had gotten on my trail so swiftly. I froze, trying to think what to do next. Then there was the sizzle of another beam, and a great limb crashed to the ground in a flurry of leaves and noise. *They were shooting into the trees!*

I tossed the stone and heard it crash into some broad-leaved plants, and crawled in the other direction as they both blasted the plants into their component atoms.

I was trapped into a stealthy crawl. To stand and run would be suicide. I crawled behind a tree and risked a look. There *were* two of them, and one was a Klingon female! She was dressed in the dark, glittery cloth that was the fashionless clothing of that strange race, and held a phaser in her hand with easy skill.

I found another stone and hefted it, waiting. When they both turned to the side to slice their blue beams into a tree, I threw the stone. It arced over their heads and rolled through the brush beyond. They both pivoted as one, their phasers firing.

I jumped to my feet and hurled my government issue Spear, Primitive, Pseudo-handcrafted, M1-A1, with all my strength.

The male Klingon took it in the back of his shoulder. He let out a terrible cry and fell thrashing into the underbrush.

The female was quick. I got behind my tree just in time. The blue beam tore off a piece of the tree next to my head. My hair stood on end from the electrical discharge, my cheek burned, and my vision was momentarily blurred as the electricity befuddled my nervous system.

She fired again, and I felt the tree shudder as the disintegrating beam cut deeply into the trunk. Another blast would get through. I flung myself away, rolling into the brush as the phaser cut into the tree trunk. The huge tree quivered and began to fall toward the Klingons, for that was the side from which the deathblow had torn a great piece from it.

As the tree fell I jumped up and ran, this time circling to their right rather than straight ahead. I heard the female Klingon cry out, and then the tree thundered to the ground. Limbs snapped, leaves showered down like green snow, and then there was silence.

I waited, breathing hard. I counted to one hundred,

then counted again. At this point it was a game of patience. She—they—were waiting, I was waiting.

I heard nothing, not even a groan. When at last the birds began to sing, I started back. I moved quietly, crouched over, fearful, without now even a primitive spear, for I had discovered my knife had disappeared in the crawling and running.

Then I saw the sprawl of black leather and maroon armor. And the shaft of my spear. The Klingon lived, but he was unconscious. It took some looking but I found the female, crushed beneath the broken branches of the great tree she had brought down on herself.

I found his phaser and cut away enough of the branches to see that she was to be no more trouble.

But there could still be other Klingons.

I walked to the ground car and radioed for an emergency vehicle, then asked for a patch to Starfleet Command. The ground ambulance had only just arrived when down came some armored assault carriers, with United States of Africa commandos, undoubtedly the first aircraft seen in the Park in over a hundred years.

■ ■ ■

Personal Log, Supplemental

I was visiting Somabula when my orders came. Incredibly, they were ordering me back to the *Enterprise*! I had just time to finish telling Somabula what the Commando colonel had told me: The Klingons had a buried ship deep in that part of the Park, from which they had planned to direct a hit-and-run terrorist group that would, they hoped, bring the world government of Earth to the breaking point.

"None of this will appear in the news reports, Commander Uhura," the colonel told me. "They'll just wait and snag each Klingon team as they get smuggled in. After two or three of their terrorist groups disappear without a trace, they'll give up.".

"Or try something else," I said, and he nodded somberly.

I said good-bye to Somabula, and we solemnly promised each other to finish the field trip another time. The mammoths were due an annual tagging, he said, and in what the press was calling "The Lost World" part of the Park, they were introducing nine different types of cloned dinosaurs to be studied *in situ* by scientists from concealed, underground laboratories.

We kissed each other a promise, and I caught a flight to Sahara. I was needed on the *Enterprise*. I don't need a reason; just being wanted aboard was enough.

A Vulcan,
A Klingon,
And An Angel

Montgomery Scott sat alone in his quarters aboard the U.S.S. *Enterprise*. Before him was an empty flask of Coridan beer, a ceramic jug of Triacus pod wine with a few drops left, and a newly opened bottle of Andorian wine-analog.

I should be drunk, Scott thought. I'm not, but I should be.

Doesn't work, not really. When you *really* want to forget, it doesn't work. Spock *is* dead and no amount of poison in my bloodstream will change that.

To distract himself, Scott flicked on a viewscreen and changed to an exterior camera. Next to them in the spacedock was the immense bulk of the newest starship in the fleet, NX 2000 *Excelsior*, a superstarship, the new Queen of Space. Loyal to the end, Scotty sniffed at the sleek lines of the great ship. Coming into spacedock, the *Enterprise*, battered and scarred, had received a standing salute from all Starfleet personnel present. Now she was docked next to the bigger ship, the new potential champion.

Transwarp drive, they said, Scotty thought moodily. Aye, but what was her *heart* like?

No ship had a heart like the *Enterprise*, he thought. *My* ship; our ship; mankind's ship.

Proven, tested, tough, been through everything there was to go through, or so it seemed. Tossed back and forth in time, teleported across the galaxy, shot at, hit, hurt, wounded, it had always come back. Once, outside the universe itself, with tantalizing glimpses of what might be other universes.

That was a concept difficult to grasp. The more one knew of *this* universe, the more one realized how huge, how complex it was. But *other* universes—?

Scott poured himself another glass of the potent wine-analog. Next to Saurian brandy, this was one of his favorites.

A wine to get lost in, at least normally. But this wasn't normal, Scott thought, this was forever. A world—a universe—without Spock.

I dinna know how much I would miss ye, Mister Spock, until ye were gone," Scott said, holding up his glass.

The annunciator chimed, and Scott frowned at the hatch. "Who is it?" he bellowed. Without waiting for an answer he grumbled, "Oh, come in."

It was an engineering trainee named Foster, a young black officer who sometimes annoyed Scott with his eagerness. "Sir? Commander Scott?"

"Yes, yes, what is it? Don't just stand there, what is it?"

"Sir, I'm Ensign Foster and—"

"I know who you are, Mister Foster. Do you think I let

anyone near my engines without knowing them all the way back to their great-grandmothers?"

"No, sir, but—"

"Then speak up. Do you want a drink?"

"No, sir, I'm on duty. Remember, you said while we're in spacedock that—"

"Yes, yes," Scott grumbled, looking into his depleted glass. "Get on with it."

"Sir, the SM-23 circuit is malfunctioning and the Dilithium Crystal 45-L is—"

"Yes, yes," Scott snapped, turning toward his screen. "Scott to Engine Room."

"Bradley, Commander."

"Pat, young Foster says the SM-23 is down."

"Yes, sir, but not to worry. I shifted to the port micro-19 and we'll have the unit out and replaced in no time."

"The 45-L? No further strain?"

"No, sir; soon as the SM-23 was off the line, it popped back to norm."

"Good work. Scott out."

Scott looked at Foster. "Why did you come by, Foster? You could have used the intercom."

Foster looked at the chronometer on Scott's desk. "I . . . I was going off duty . . . I am off duty in thirty seconds, and I thought . . . uh . . . I wondered . . ."

"Say it, Ensign. You don't have time for hemmin' and hawin' around here."

"Sir, I . . . well, I know Mister Spock was very important, and it's always terrible to lose a leader but, well, I mean, we know the risks. He *did* die a hero and—"

"Mister Foster!" Commander Scott's voice cut in with

an icy edge. He started to speak, and then his expression changed to one of great weariness.

"Sit down, Mister Foster." He shoved a glass toward the youth and sloshed some Andorian wine-analog into it. "Sit," he ordered. "You're off duty now, and a man should not drink to absent friends alone."

Stiffly, the young officer eased himself into a chair and picked up the glass. He sniffed, made a face, and took a sip. His eyes blinked open and he swallowed hard.

"To Mister Spock," Scott said.

"To, uh, to Mister Spock," Foster said, gingerly sipping the wine.

Scott stared at the youth long enough to make the young engineer nervous. "So," Scott said at last, "you want to know why Spock's dying has made us all so gloomy?"

"No, sir. I mean, yes, sir; no, uh, well, it's just that—"

"You ever lose anyone, Foster? Someone *close*? Real close?" Scott took another swallow as Foster muttered a nervous answer.

"Well, um, my grandfather, sir. He died in a mine cave-in on the Moon when I was a boy. And I had an uncle aboard the *Lydia Marano* when she got caught by that black hole."

"Well, Mister Spock was no grandfather and he died saving us all, including you. But he was already a hero. He didn't have to die to prove that. A hero a dozen times over, a *hundred* times. Did you ever hear about him and the angel?"

Foster blinked, his eyes watering from another sip of wine-analog. "Uh, no, sir. An *angel*, sir? You mean, uh, like from Heaven, that kind of, uh, angel?"

Scott nodded solemnly. "An angel," h.
"Not that kind of angel, but maybe as close
in this world." Scott laughed, and waved his
in this world, boy. You know, I think I *am* gett.
Good." He picked up the bottle and filled Foste
much to the youth's dismay. "Drink and I'll t you
about Mister Spock, the Klingon king, and the angel."

■ ■ ■

It was on our first voyage, Scott said. A year out,
maybe a little more. We all knew each other, though
Chekov hadn't been promoted up to the bridge yet.
Things were settled in, or getting there. We'd met that
rogue Harry Mudd, and Kevin Riley had had his run; the
captain had bluffed them with the Corbomite maneuver
and we'd discovered Kodos the Executioner and had a
brush with the Romulans. Mister Spock had helped out
Captain Pike, and we'd had a run-in with the cursed
Squire of Gothos. We'd all survived a most curious shore
leave, and the captain had fought the Gorn. It happened
about then.

There was this little settlement on a backwater world
called Alva. Edison II it was, a little two-world system
near the Klingon line. Thomas and Alva, they were the
planets. Cute, huh? Never know what people are going
to call things, do you? Some like the classics: Athos,
Plato, Capricorn. Some like naming things after the folks
who paid for the trip. The Spaniards used to do that
when they were exploring the New World. Name things
for saints' days and queens, kings. Christmas Island, San
Francisco, you know them?

Well, sometimes they get too cute, know what I mean?

But you *never* have people calling their planet by the legal terminology. Would you recognize SSL-1833-VI? That's the 1,833 star listed in the Starfleet Star List, the sixth planet thereof. Which is it? Don't know, do you? Not that way, but say Ulysses and you know, right? Sixth world of Homer. People don't like numbers, they like names.

I've gotten off the track. Spock, right. We went over to Alva, on of those Starfleet services no one ever notices. Too far out it was for commercial freighters, so when we go from point A to point B, we try to stop in, see how things are, offload stores, medicines, check things out. Routine. Usually routine. Not this time.

Have some more wine, Foster. No? Then some good Triacus pod wine? Good stuff. You'll develop a taste, we'll see to that. No use going out and risking your neck and losing good people like Mister Spock and not getting some of the advantages, is there? The potato, for instance. Tomato. Corn. Philarda. Grizmalt. Lassfass. All good stuff, in their way. All brought from new worlds to old.

Alva, right. Tiny little Terran colony there. Commercial colony planted, oh, fifty, sixty years before by an investment group on Earth. Stock bought and sold. Glamour stock, y'know. "Our colony on Edison II," that kind of chitchat. Like people talking about "their Broadway show."

Broadway? New York, you know. Before tri-D. Live drama, musical? Never mind. There we were, Mister Spock, Doctor McCoy, and me, beaming down. The doctor to check out the medical things, me to see if they needed any technological help—you know, copying out some manuals, tech stuff from the library, show 'em how to repair things. Mister Spock, he was to do a culture check. Know how a doctor will take your temperature, a bloodtest? Well, Spock, he was to look over the culture, like. Sometimes these little isolated colonies get right off the track. Petty tyrants evolve, maybe they actually mutate because of bacteria or radiation that got missed during the initial survey. Once we found a colony of Terrans that had completely forgotten about Earth or America or anything. Still went by the Constitution, though—even if they only had a few fragments of it left.

Anyway, there we were. Captain Kirk took the *Enterprise* over to Thomas, up close to the sun, which kind of complicated things, as you'll see, because the solar wind was so strong we couldn't radio them.

Oh, forgot: coupla security men beamed down, too, and Pat Bradley. Yup, same Pat as is down in the engine room right now.

Everything looked just fine. We always beam down—if time permits—just a bit out from where the people are. Especially those without much technology, or primitives. Don't like to scare folks. So there we were, and there was this village, and out steps a whole squad of Klingons!

"Don't move," Spock said. There were too many of them, nearly twice as many, and they had their phasers on us. I was so angry I could have chewed dilithium crystals!

No reason to expect them, no ship on the screens as we came in. Life forms, sure, but they were all mixed in with the colonists.

Ambushed. Our weapons were taken away and we were trapped. The Klingons had us, they had the colonists, but we didn't know what they were up to.

Of course, we knew that pretty soon the *Enterprise* would be back, and there's no Klingon ship can best her. Isn't that right, baby?

I'm talking to the *Enterprise*, Mister Foster, who did you think?

But, y'see, we had to survive. I guess that's where the angel came in.

See, we ran the records coming into orbit. What all the other Starfleet ships had reported on Alva. Remarkable record: no fights, no revolutions, no strife worth noting. Yet nothing was run from the top, as if some despot had taken over. Just good folks living together in peace. Remarkable, in a way, but hardly unique. Guess that's another reason we came in so blind. Nothing had ever happened before. There were no animals that were dangerous except humans, and they had this record of peace.

So, as I said, the Klingons had us and the top dog among 'em was this Klandor. Called himself a king, but I think it's a bit like the Irish—all descended from kings, they say. Insisted we call him Your Majesty and such. Obnoxious fellow, but so are all Klingons. Do it just to be nasty, sometimes even to their own disadvantage, I think.

Klandor was up to something, we knew that. It was Mister Spock who figured it out. "They will force us to signal the ship to beam them aboard, threatening to kill the colonists if we do not," he said. They'd be holding the communicators, you see, and automatically the transporter beams would take them up, and they'd go in firing.

It was Spock who figured the rest out as well. The Klingons knew we were in the area—we weren't exactly sneaking around, and Starfleet likes to remind the Klingons we have ships all over. So they knew our policy and figured we'd drop in on Alva sooner or later.

So we had to trust that Captain Kirk would be able to decipher this code word that Spock planned to slip in. Didn't work that way. We didn't know it, but as the Klingons were interrogating us they had been making recordings and they had put together messages from each of us that would fool our voice decoders because they would *be* our voices.

But Klandor was smart—or so he thought. He sent up Spock in the front, backed up by Klandor and five Klingons. That moment before the transporter crew got up the nerve to fire into a group of Klingons with Mister Spock standing in front was the crucial few moments.

Only none of it happened that way. Oh, the *Enterprise* came back and the voice recordings worked and they beamed up Spock, Klandor, and the six assault troops.

And nothing happened. At least nothing seemed to happen. They didn't arrive. We never *did* find out what happened to the six troopers, but Mister Spock and this Klandor got somewhere. Limbo, Spock called it. A nothingness.

There they were, alive and well and in nowhere land. Spock and Klandor and the angel. Of course Spock isn't of any religion that has angels in it, but he does know about them. Klandor . . . well, to him it was some kind of winged creature—yes, Foster, big white feathery wings—and that's it. Spock said there was no halo. But then, I don't think angels have halos; at least this one didn't. The halos you see in paintings are the invention of medieval artists.

A Vulcan, a Klingon, and an angel.

No, Foster, I *don't* think I should like down and sleep. Mister Spock is lying down and asleep and he'll be forgotten if everyone lies down and goes to sleep, doncha see?

I know, Foster, they're gonna give him the highest award, the United Federation of Planets Golden Medal of Honor. Posthumous, of course. But I'm telling you of when he was *alive*, when he was *Spock*!

A Vulcan, a Klingon, and an angel.

How do I know? 'Cause I was there when he reported to Captain Kirk and when it was sent to Starfleet and when Starfleet put a cap on it. It won't be in the records, son. Some things just aren't. Starfleet policy, y'know. Have some more wine, boy.

All in limbo. The Klingon, of course, he went on the attack right off. With one of them Klingon roars, he charged Spock like an animal. But Spock was cool and tossed him. The Klingon, he came again and just knocked Spock down and tried to strangle him, but Spock got his hands inside Klandor's arms and broke the hold and flipped the Klingon off. They were about to go at it again when the angel said, "Stop."

They stopped. Just like that. Spock realized the voice was in his head. Telepathy, you know. Not uncommon, though very few from Earth seem to have it. Stopped 'em dead, it did. Oh, shouldn't have said that. Not dead. They, they stopped, is all.

The angel said . . . well, telepathed . . . oh, blast, the angel *said*, in their minds, "Opposites do not attract, they repel when dealing with life forms."

The Klingon, he tried to attack the angel, but he took

only one step, Spock said, and he couldn't go any farther. Like a wall was there. Didn't faze the angel. Are angels hes or shes, Foster? Supposed to be neutral, aren't they, but what about Saint Michael and . . . oh, I'm off the subject again. Here, I need more wine. You, Foster?

So, well, there they were. The angry Klingon—I don't think they come in any other type—and the cool Vulcan and the neutral angel. Great winged creature, white robe, the whole works. Symbol of Goodness, but maybe an absence of Evil and an absence of Good, a lack of emotion, would make us think of someone like that as "good." Spock, he had emotions. Oh, he tried to hide it. He was ashamed of emotions, you know. Half-Terran, half-Vulcan, he had emotions and he fought always to hide them. Except maybe to the Captain. He was loyal, you know. He believed in what we are doing out there in space, seeking intelligence, finding order, extending our knowledge. Pour me some of that, will you, Foster? Good lad.

Spock's dead, you know that, Foster? Dead. On the Genesis planet. Dead saving us all. You, me, everyone. People ought to know a man like Spock. Great man, Mister Spock.

Hey? Oh, yes. The angel and the Klingon and Mister Spock. Good, Evil, and Neutral. The angel said, "The classic confrontation." Spock was probably the first to undertand. Good against Evil, with the stakes high. But how high? Were they to fight for their own futures? For the *Enterprise* and Alva? For the future of mankind or Klingonkind? Spock did not know, only that there was to be a battle.

"The limbo grew vast," he said, Spock said. "It became

a vast plain, gray and neutral, with white lines making a vast grid. Squares of the grid rose and fell, becoming obstructions, hills, mountains; other sections became pits, holes, canyons. And they changed, up and down, some slowly, some abruptly." He told us with a kind of cool wonder and he said he had tried to analyze the mechanism, but he didn't have the information and he didn't have the time.

The Klingon attacked. The angel had the floor or ground or whatever it was drop away from beneath, but he or she or it just hovered there, watching. The Klingon knocked Spock down, but they both fell, and when they rolled to their feet there was a gully of depressed squares between them and cliffs behind. Changing square columns of cliffs rippling as they rose and fell like some great biological pipe organ. The gully leveled off and the Klingon came on, but the squares rose, carrying the Klingon up. He leaped off, but Spock dodged him, striking a solid blow.

Spock knew that it was a matter of life and death and the stakes were unknown but high. He had dealt the Klingon a mighty blow, enough to kill a man, yet the Klingon lay still only for a moment, then rose. "I knew we were not functioning under the normal laws of space and time," Spock told us. "We could not be killed—or rather, we could be killed but instantly repaired."

"The Metrons," Captain Kirk had said later. We all nodded. They're a mysterious race, who put Captain Kirk against the Gorn on a lifeless asteroid with their races as the prize. The winner's race lived, the loser's died. It didn't work out quite like that, but those were the stakes, y'see, Foster.

"But they were not the Metrons," Spock said, and again we all agreed, since the Metrons had kept themselves invisible to us. The angel was seen, the angel was physical.

"We could have gone on fighting forever," Spock said. "Gaining and losing the advantage. I sought an answer, but the Klingon kept attacking. It is difficult to be logical while you are engaging in basic survival."

Captain Kirk and I smiled at each other over that. How like Spock to be coolly logical during a life-and-death struggle. "I knew," he told us, "that I must find the key. Perhaps we were entertainment for this winged creature and nothing more. So in moments out of combat—that is, as we gathered strength to attack each other again—I spoke to this astonishing life form."

Y'see, that was so like Spock. Foster, your glass is empty, lad. So Spock says, "Are you an angel?" The creature says, "I am as I appear."

"Could you change your appearance?" Spock asked, and the creature does not respond, but this did catch the attention of the Klingon, amazingly enough. "What are you?" bellowed Klandor. "How dare you toy with Klandor!"

The Klingon went on like this for some time. All emotional and egotistic, Spock says, but it gave him time to think. "King Klandor," Spock says with great solemnity, "I perceive we are engaging in combat under false pretenses."

"Any opportunity to kill a Vulcan or their pet dogs, the Earthmen, is a welcome opportunity," the Klingon said.

"Even if it makes a fool of you?" Spock asked, and the

Klingon roared and was about to attack again. The landscape shifted again and a crevass appeared between them, then began to reverse itself and fill in, the square gray columns rising. As the Klingon waited, he apparently thought. They are a crafty lot, the Klingons, and suspicious. They see treachery everywhere, the galaxy is against them. But their egos are so big it makes them vulnerable.

"No one makes a fool of King Klandor!" the Klingon bellowed.

"This creature is making a fool of us both," Spock said. "It assumes the form of an angel, a creature of myth, a religious icon, to confuse us. We are pawns for its pleasure."

The Klingon growled and stared hotly at the angel. The white wings fluttered and folded and darkened as they looked. The pale skin reddened, a pointed tail grew, horns grew, and before their eyes it became a traditional devil, with pointed ears and slanted eyes like a Vulcan . . . and like a Klingon, too, for that matter.

The devil laughed. "I am everything, everyone, every race. I am Good and Evil and whatever I wish." Then it changed, each form flowing into the next, a devil, to a likeness of a mature Klingon, to a Romulan, to something shapeless and green with weaving tentacles to a winged Pegasus to a human female to an Andorian Alpha to Captain Kirk to Kang, one of the Klingon leaders.

"What are you?" Klandor yelled. Spock said the Klingon was afraid, but had courage in defying whatever it was.

"I am your mind, Klingon, and you, Vulcan. I am your deepest thoughts, the creature from you reptile brains, the thing that crawled from the warm salt oceans. I am Fear, I am Death."

"You are a child," Spock said. "You are none of those things. You are Ego. You toy with those of lesser powers like a cat with a mouse. You are a bully."

The creature grew larger, looming over them, a dark horned and clawed creature neither could identify. The Klingon caught on fast. "Yes, you are a nest warden, petty and tyrannical, a poor substitute for a clan leader!"

Spock drilled in hard. "A petty tyrant who bullies children! An illogical creature who fears the world of logical adults!"

The creature changed again—to a Terran bull, a Vegan wart-worm, a giant scorpion-analog, a Vulcan legged snake, an ogre from children's fantasies. But both the Klingon and Spock stood against it, whipping it into a frenzy with their biting comments and insults.

The creature fired bolts of lightning off into the boiling skies. The gray plain rippled and cracked. Impossible spires shot into the sky and deep crevasses split the surface. The sleek, crisp edges of the square columns crumbled and rotted, revealing a dull black interior, which boiled and writhed.

"Bully!" shouted Spock. "Egotistical and immature!"

The Klingon shouted insults in Klingonese, and the creature shrank.

It reversed itself, back through all the personas it had assumed, back through the white-winged angel, back through humanoid and alien shapes, shrinking, dissolving. The gray plain, too, changed, back to the neutral limbo, back to a shabby, ill-defined surface, an asteroid world with foul-smelling air.

Then the creature stopped changing. It was a small creature, weak-limbed and pale, with a large head and large, dark eyes.

"Send us back," the Klingon demanded.

"You're no fun," the creature said.

"Pick on someone your own size!" the Klingon snarled.

"There *is* no one my size!" the creature said petulantly.

But Spock was still curious. That was our Spock, Foster, eternally curious. Spock said, "What is your name?" The thing did not respond. "From what planet, what race?"

"No. You'll tell on me."

"Send us back!" roared the Klingon. *"I have Earthmen to kill!"*

"Oh, very well. But you'll never find me. You'll never punish me!" The creature disappeared then. Just *poof!* gone. Then the Klingon just went away, and Spock, too, and they found themselves arriving on the *Enterprise*, on the transporter deck. And Spock recovered first, knocking out the Klingons with his Vulcan nerve pinch before any of them knew what was happening.

What happened then? Well, lad, we put the Klingons back on Alva, but we had to build a prison for them. Sooner or later a Klingon ship would come by and they'd be released.

Now you ask, why had that Earth colony been so peaceful? It had been a trap. It had amused the angel—or whatever you want to call it—to control the life forms there. Perhaps it knew no others. When the warlike Klingons arrived, it saw an opportunity for entertainment.

Yes, it *was* a child. Of sorts. One who does not understand responsibility of power or leadership and only used its powers to entertain itself. Someday it will mature and use its considerable powers constructively.

A moral, Foster? Yes, a moral. Power without responsibility is madness, just as responsibility without power is useless.

Why, yes, Foster, you may refill my glass. A toast, then. To Mister Spock! Wherever he is.

World's
End

"**P**arking orbit completed, Captain," Sulu stated. He glanced over his right shoulder at Admiral James T. Kirk, who nodded brusquely.

"Report, Mister Spock," the captain said.

"Life forms detected, Captain. A few score, is my guess, no more, and deep down." The Vulcan turned to look at Kirk. "May I remind you, Captain, we must report to Base IV in three days' time."

"Yes, Spock, I know," Kirk said patiently, then grinned. "But how often do you find a world completely covered by a building hundreds of stories deep? And abandoned?

"Never, sir, as far as the library reports. It is a unique situation. But we still must get the medicines to Starbase IV."

"We have thirty hours' leeway, Mister Spock. I propose a few hours exploring this unique situation. Is there any indication of its racial origin?"

"None detectable from space, sir. The construction is

standard. It seems to vary from three to seven hundred feet deep. A strong but not unusual steel alloy was employed. The variation in depth might indicate an underlying terrain. The outer surface is varied, with starship locks, domes, towers, and other unremarkable markings all over it. Logic indicates a highly developed industrial world which has been abandoned, or devastated by some plague. I do not suggest exploration, Captain Kirk."

"Spock, Spock," Kirk said with amusement. "A mystery world and you don't want us to unravel the mystery?"

"May I remind the captain of the necessity to arrive on time at Base IV?"

"Yes, yes, but none of the ships will be leaving to distribute their cargoes to the Moradaine System until *all* the Federation ships arrive with their cargoes. There are four others besides us, Mister Spock. Caladral vaccine from Regulus, aboard the *Hood*. Triasphal and megathormal on the *Republic*. The *Steven Barnes* has the biotynes and the medical assault teams. The *Tajarhi* has the menaprophyne, I believe. None of these things is effective without the other. We have time, a little time. I am not being irresponsible, am I?" He said it with a smile, and Spock raised his eyebrows.

"No, Captain. It is my duty to remind you of such things."

"It will be noted in the log, Mister Spock. Now, would you care to accompany me down to the surface?" Spock nodded, and Kirk looked at the young Russian, Chekov. "Mister Chekov, you have the conn." Kirk punched the intercom. "Doctor McCoy, meet me in the transporter room."

■ ■ ■

"Sir, the transporter beam is set for the sixth level down, which is the first section sealed against the vacuum," the transporter officer said.

"Air is good?" Kirk asked.

"We sent down a scoop, sir, while you were on the way from the bridge. The computer reports it within defined limits of breathable atmosphere for humans. And, uh, Vulcans, too, Mister Spock."

Spock only raised an eyebrow. Doctor McCoy entered briskly. "What's going on, Jim? I have a couple of crewmen in sick bay who—"

"Anything critical, Bones?"

"No, an allergic reaction to some Coridan melbar—God only knows where she got it—and a good old-fashioned case of Centaurian flu."

"Doctor Chapel can handle it, then?"

"Yes, of course, but—"

"Prepare to go ashore, Doctor McCoy. That *is* your kitbag, isn't it?"

"Yes, Jim, and a Mark IV Feinberger, too, but—"

"Lieutenant Collins?"

"My men are ready," the security officer reported.

"Where's Bradley? Ah."

"Sorry, sir," the young engineering officer said as he ran into the transporter room. "I was helping Commander Scott recalibrate the Three-Thirteen logistic circuit and—"

"Time for some hands-on experience, Mister Bradley."

At Pat Bradley's puzzled frown, Kirk smiled. "I have a habit of using archaic phrases from the dawn of the Age of Technology, mister. Hands-on: practical experience, not texttape theorizing. You would be amazed at the difference. Would he, Mister Spock?"

"Yes, Captain. Reality is often more complex than theorizing. Nothing is as clear-cut and precise."

"You just hate that, don't you, Spock?" McCoy said with a grin as they climbed onto the transporter stage.

"I accept, Doctor McCoy, that is true. It makes for interesting variations."

"Ready?" Kirk asked. "Energize!"

The landing party shimmered as the transporter beams scanned their bodies. They glittered and vibrated and were gone.

■ ■ ■

The space they materialized in was large and desolate and bitter cold. There was a mist of frost on the blotched metal walls. It had once been some kind of manufacturing area, with blocks and raised platforms all about, with bolt holes and rusting freezelock pediments where machinery had once been attached.

"Scouts out," Kirk ordered, and two of the red-jacketed security men moved ahead and two dropped behind. In the main party were Kirk, Spock, McCoy, Bradley, and Tom Collins, the security lieutenant.

They moved into a corridor, bleak and cold, and Spock consulted his tricorder. "Life-form readings this way, Captain."

They went down a ramp, turned along a passage and down another set of stairs. Deeper and deeper they went, passing through airlocks and rusting hatches. It became progressively warmer. They went down a non-functioning escalator and stopped.

"What conclusions have you drawn, Mister Spock" Kirk asked.

"By the width of the passages and the height of the steps, I calculate a large race, on the order of three meters, or about half again the usual humanoid size. By the placement of controls, I estimate large, four-fingered hands. You'll notice that decorations, button placement, and architectural design is on multiples of four. Common enough; humanoids with their ten fingers base everything from mathematics to games on ten."

"Hostile or friendly?" Kirk asked.

"Unknown, Captain. Insufficient data. I would say they were perhaps bureaucrats."

McCoy raised his eyebrows. "How do you determine that?"

"A world covered with a building indicates a highly centralized civilization. They are technological, of course, and quite sophisticated in that way, but you'll have noticed the near absence of artistic decoration. Methodical minds, and perhaps even hivelike."

"Logical?" McCoy said with a faint smile.

"Logic dictates a rational approach to goals, Doctor McCoy. Just as the eye needs resting places amid chaos, so does the mind. Art in its many forms are 'resting places' for the intellect, Doctor. Therefore even the illogical products of art serve a logical function. Do you have any other comments, Doctor McCoy?"

McCoy flushed and shook his head. Kirk said, "Hivelike, Spock? Like bees, ants, ranothrax, and so on?"

Spock nodded. "It's possible, Captain. With an average depth of thirty-five hundred feet and the estimated size of the world beneath, I would say the volume of the buildings is large enough to cover North and South America with a building nine stories deep."

"Whew!" Lieutenant Collins said in amazement.

"And a few dozen life forms?" McCoy said. "It's virtually a dead world. Let's hope whatever caused it to be deserted is not still here."

"We have twenty-nine hours left, gentlemen," Kirk said. "Shall we continue?"

■ ■ ■

They were down fourteen floors before they encountered any sign of life. It was on a tattered strip of cloth. McCoy's Feinberger detected harmless bacteria, but it *was* the first sign of any life.

Two floors down they encountered the first life form: a rat. Not exactly a Terran rat, but a rodentlike creature the size of a mouse, gray and scaly. It scampered away into the darkness out of the exploring party's lights, humming rather than squeaking.

The next life form was something more substantial: a genuine inhabitant. "A moment, Captain," Spock cautioned, looking at his tricorder. "I detect something ahead, around that corridor. It's—"

There was a flicker of movement and, even as phasers were drawn, a pale ray enveloped them. The men grunted as they fell. Spock was the last to fall, and his phaser's beam caroomed off the metal walls as he fired.

There was silence. The lights lay on the metal flooring, canted and making strange shadows on the wall. Then something moved slowly out of the darkness and crept closer.

A four-fingered hand reached through the light beam to tug at a body. Slowly the body was pulled out of the tangle of limbs and dragged away into the darkness.

Mister Spock had been selected.

■ ■ ■

Kirk flipped open his communicator. His head ached and he felt stiff and twitchy. A reaction of his nervous system to whatever had downed them, McCoy had said. He was bandaging the bleeding cut on one of the security women's head.

"*Enterprise*, come in, this is Kirk." He stared at the device moodily. "How come there's never a starship around when you need one? Collins!"

"Yes, sir!" The lieutenant was right at Kirk's side.

"Report!"

"Except for Kuntz's head, everyone is all right, barring headaches. Mister Spock has disappeared. We've scouted the immediate area, and detect no one. Mister Spock's tricorder is gone, too, sir."

"Collins, give Kuntz a message and have her climb back to where the communicator can penetrate all this metal. Report to the ship what has happened and that we are proceeding deeper. Have two assault teams in full armor beamed down. Tell them we'll leave a four-ten radiation trail for them to follow."

"The trail of breadcrumbs," Collins grinned, then sobered. "Yes, sir, at once!"

■ ■ ■

Spock came to slowly. He was being dragged along by one leg, his head and body bouncing over trash and distortions in the metal floor. He could barely see the creature who was pulling him along as casually as a child's wagon. If they went down some stairs, the Vulcan was not sure he would survive.

He moaned loudly to attract attention, and faked a limp posture. The creature stopped and looked back. In the dim light from a wall lamp—the first he had seen— Spock made out the hulking giant who held his ankle in a grip of steel.

There was some satisfaction in noting that he had diagnosed the approximate size. The thing was about three meters high, but not humanoid. It was barrel-shaped, with long, thick, powerful arms. It was bipedal but not humanoid, for the thick legs were like those of an elephant. The head was large, tapering to a thick snout not unlike an anteater. It was hairy and gray-green and had small, suspicious eyes. It did not look friendly.

Spock groaned again and feebly moved his limbs, faking a weakness. The response was more than Spock expected. The creature picked him up as easily as a baby and slung the Vulcan across its broad shoulders. Spock struggled, but the huge creature simply pulled Spock around and struck him in the side of the head, then reslung the limp body of the Vulcan over its shoulder.

■ ■ ■

Kirk's team walked deeper and deeper into the world-spanning building. Every few feet, or at every turning, Collins "drew" on the metal walls with a low-radiation device, leaving a trail invisible except under ultraviolet light.

"Come on," urged Kirk at every hesitation. "Spock may be in trouble."

■ ■ ■

"Mister Chekov, a communication from the surface," Uhura said.

"Chekov here," the young Russian said, thumbing the switch.

"Commander, this is Kuntz, Corporal Natasha Kuntz, I have a message from Captain Kirk."

Chekov listened to the message, his face tightening with concern. "How many levels did you have to climb to get us?" he asked.

"Up to the eleventh, sir. This metal must be more dense than it looks."

"Establish a command post there, Kuntz." Chekov thumbed another stud. "Security, two combat teams on the double! Full battle gear, prepare to be beamed down at once! Mister Spock has been . . . Mister Spock is missing. Beam in on Corporal Kuntz's transmission!"

Chekov signed off and stole a concerned look at Uhura. They exchanged meaningful glances. They had been there before, but both were fully aware that *this* time might bring disaster to their friends. Uhura smiled reassuringly.

Chekov looked at the screen. They were holding stationary over the turning metal world, right over where Kirk and his team had penetrated the vast structure.

Would the world become an immense tombstone for Kirk, Spock, and the others?

■ ■ ■

Spock regained consciousness lying on a slab. It was cold in the room, but all Vulcans can bear up under cold better than most humans. He looked around as another part of his mind checked over his body.

Headache. Bruise on side of head. Otherwise unharmed.

Equipment check. Still clothed. Communicator still in belt but both phaser and tricorder gone.

Spock sat up. Had he lost the tricorder while being dragged? The phaser he remembered in his hand as he was felled under the pale beam. Undoubtedly dropped at that point. He pulled out the communicator, but as he suspected, all he got was static. He replaced it and looked around.

Bare metal room with high ceiling, wide tall door, no furniture but a slab jutting from the wall opposite the door. Blank smooth area on side wall, no visible controls.

Head pounding, Spock stood up. He blanked out the pain and crossed to the wall. He pressed the wall all around the smooth area, but nothing happened.

"Activate," he said. Nothing happened. "Start. Begin. Open." He quickly ran through similar commands in several languages of the Federation, then in Klingon, Romulan, and Sarcaniflex. No response.

Spock thought a moment. Perhaps it was not a screen, but he had no idea what else it might be, as it was not reflective enough to be a mirror. It might be one-way, a kind of sign or calling device, activated from the exterior.

He turned his attention to the large door. There was a cross-shaped knob, suitable for a four-fingered hand, but it would not turn. Spock walked to the slab, sat upon it cross-legged, and started to meditate.

■ ■ ■

The gray corridor opened into a vast hall, and Kirk heard scampering across the great space, echoing sharply. A few hums and scratchings, and then silence. Beams from the lights of Collins' team swept the room.

It was a vast, bowl-shaped room with a raised center platform. And skeletons. Hundreds of them. Some whole, in clusters, some broken and scattered. Where breaks had happened, the bones were almost shattered into dust.

"Look at that," McCoy said, pointing to a nearby skeleton that was virtually whole. The structure was immense, more than nine feet long, with thick, sturdy legs and hipbones. A great jawbone sagged open beneath a skull like a bison but with a long, sharp, beaklike protrudence.

Its only garment was the fragile, dry, rotting straps of some kind of harness. There were no weapons, no sign of why the creature had died.

"Are these the inhabitants, or invaders, or . . . or *pets?*" Kirk asked. They walked toward the center of the room, a vast graveyard full of unburied bodies. Here and there they saw smaller skeletons, almost as big as a human, but compared to the adult whatever-they-were, they had to be children.

They crossed the room and continued a short distance, then Kirk called a halt. "They could have taken any number of turnings," he said. "We could get lost ourselves, except for the trail of crumbs."

"Captain," Pat Bradley said. "Could I make a suggestion?" Kirk gestured for him to go on. "Someone or some *thing* took Mister Spock. He must have had a reason. Why him? Why not you or me or one of the others? He *was* the only Vulcan, sir."

"You may have something, Bradley. Spock was the last to go down. I saw him out of the corner of my eye as I passed out. Perhaps that attracted whoever or whatever took him."

"Sir, I hate to say this, but, uh, there could be cannibalism here, sir," Collins said. "Place like this, no sign of food growing. We know there are *some* people here; at least something's alive here."

"A distasteful but logical thought, Tom. All those bones."

"They weren't eaten, Jim," McCoy said. "At least not by carnivores or omnivores. Bugs, maybe, ants, that kind of thing. No teeth marks or limbs torn off." Kirk gave an involuntary twitch, and he wasn't the only one. "No, they died from something nonviolent and just rotted away."

"Perhaps that is what killed off the original inhabitants," Bradley said.

"Sir, Mister Spock thought this might be a bureaucratic world, a kind of star center." Kirk nodded. "Then there would be ships coming in from all over, perhaps even from new planets."

"There were no ships in the docking spots outside," Kirk mused. "All gone. Indicating perhaps that the survivors fled."

McCoy moaned. "Spreading the disease everywhere!"

"People in fear of their life don't always think rationally," Kirk said. "Good theory, Bradley. As good as any."

"Um, sir?" one of the nearby security men said. "Does, uh, does that mean *we* might get whatever it was?" Kirk looked to McCoy.

"Perhaps. Some microorganisms can last a phenomenally long time. But my guess is that it does not. However, if there are survivors, it must mean that they are either immune or have some kind of protection. In which case we could get it from *them*." He looked at Kirk. "Or Spock could."

■ ■ ■

At the first sound of someone at the door, Spock's slanted eyes popped open. The metal door squeaked open, and the creature who had captured him stood there. Or at least a genetic duplicate. The great gray-green creature barked a command in a language Spock did not recognize, but the gesture told him enough.

The lean Vulcan rose from the protruding slab and walked out the door, past the towering hulk of his captor. In the corridor were two other of the creatures. Each had a harness of metal links from which hung a squarish weapon of some kind and a short sword. They flanked Spock and started off down the passage.

It was a maze through which they passed, a series of rusting rooms without much ornamentation or comfort. Spock saw improvised beds and fires tended by ancient bent figures, older duplicates of his captors. He saw no children or any less than full-grown Alphas, as he had named them.

At times their trail led through rents in walls, blackened holes blasted through in some ancient time. They skirted a great dark well so vast he could not see the other side. Here and there on the walls or ceilings were dim lights, just enough to navigate by.

It was a dreary, dead place, unexciting, without, Spock thought, the austere grandness of Vulcan habitations. It was a worn-out world, with a weary, worn-out population, gray and shabby.

Then they came upon a great hatch upon which was crudely welded a kind of shield. There were symbols on the shield: concentric circles, a bar with a disk at one end, and what Spock took to be a four-winged bird.

The concentric circles seemed to Spock to be a representation of the multi-layer structure which covered the unnamed planet, but the other symbols' meanings he could not interpret.

The hatch was guarded by two of the gray-green Alphas, each with a rod of metal sharpened at one end. They tugged on the hatch manually, and it creaked open enough for Spock's guards to squeeze through.

At once Spock was assaulted by a great variety of sensual stimulants: warm, moist air rather than the cold, dry, tasteless air outside; bright light, tending toward the red end of the scale; the sound of stringed instruments playing atonal music; and smells unlike any he had experienced.

What he saw was a vast, low-ceilinged chamber populated with circular gazebos, round, shiny, metal balls the size of a room, disks set a foot or so off the floor, which was carpeted with groupings of round, shiny, wet-looking rugs. And in and about these objects were about a dozen creatures of a totally different genetic heritage from the gray-green hulks who had brought Spock there.

They were vaguely reptilian about the face, but their bodies were almost catlike, sleek and supple. They had tails with tufts of hair at the end, and the hair was treated differently by each of the creatures: braided, fluffed into fuzzy balls, oiled and shaped into glistening spirals, and so on.

All the creatures wore jewelry: silvery bands carved and jeweled, necklaces of polished metal shapes, earrings of braided wires, belts of linked metal shapes, needles of golden metal glued in sprays around the eyes.

And all eyes were unblinkingly upon Spock. Two Alphas pushed Spock forward toward one of the new aliens, which Spock was already calling Betas in his mind. The nomenclature was simple, usable until real names were discovered.

This Beta was lying on a pallet of ornamented pillows, and as Spock approached, he or she—the Vulcan could not tell which—picked up a bar with a sphere on top, which started to glow the moment it was touched.

Spock was stopped by an Alpha on each side, and the leader on the round pallet said something to the Vulcan in a hissing voice. When Spock did not reply, the Beta made a gesture and the two Alphas knocked Spock to the floor.

The Vulcan science officer lay still for a moment, feigning unconsciousness, and tried to sort out the impressions. *A deserted metal world. Two very different races, with the physically stronger the slaves or servants of the other. A few overlords living in luxury upon the labor of the subjected. A dead-end, depleted, autocratic society. And where is Jim Kirk?*

The Alphas yanked Spock to his feet and the Beta leader spoke again. But this time Spock responded. "I am Spock, Science Officer of the United Federation of Planets ship *Enterprise*. We have come in peace and—"

The Beta leader raised this sphere-on-a-rod and pointed it at Spock and everything went black. *Click*. No flash, no sound, no fading of powers, just blackness. No sensation at all.

Fascinating, Spock thought. *Instantaneous neurological disconnection. Yet I can still think. Only the input of my senses has malfunctioned. Very little sense of time. I am thinking, and even thinking requires time, therefore time is passing. I cannot be dead; this is not death.*

Spock waited a moment, searching his mind for the slightest sign of sensory input, and found none. *Very well. I will attempt an analysis of the biological functioning of the Betas from information available to me. After that, if the malfunctioning has not ceased, I shall run the Paradoxes of Nome-kre-all.*

Actually, Spock thought, *this is a most unusual circumstance, one to explore. An electronically induced state of nothingness, a powered meditation.*

Having determined there was nothing he could do to change his state of being, Spock decided to employ it.

▪ ▪ ▪

Kirk held up his hand. Ahead of him the security man serving as scout had given him a warning sign, then motioned them closer.

Around the angle of a corridor Kirk saw a lumbering creature, gray-green and hulking. The alien went into a room, and from it Kirk saw a flickering fire. They crept closer, and Kirk could see a bent figure sitting by a fire with the other figure standing nearby. The fire itself was of interest: raggedly torn sheets of some carpetlike material glowing fitfully but not actually in flames.

Kirk motioned them back. As they started to retreat for a conference, one of the security men scuffed his boot on some of the grit on the floor.

With a roar the gray-green giant rushed out, a terrifying figure three meters tall. Three stun beams hit him at once, and the hulk fell across Pat Bradley with a crash.

Immediately Tom Collins rushed into the fire-lit room and hit the old creature with a stunbeam. He carefully laid the bent figure out flat, then returned to help Bradley to his feet.

"Captain, look," one of the security men said. There was a well-defined path through the grit and rubble, out of the room through a hole smashed in the wall. On the edge of the ragged tear in the metal was caught Spock's tricorder.

"This way!" Kirk said at once. "Tom, tell the follow-up teams where we're going."

"Yes, sir," the security lieutenant said, writing across the metal wall with the marking beam.

■ ■ ■

From blackness to full sensory awareness in an instant. Sight, sound, smell, everything returned at once. It was like a blow to Spock's mind, but he immediately attempted to re-orient himself.

He was lying on the round carpets before the Beta leader's platform. *Seconds or hours?* Spock wondered. He saw the reptilian head of the leader pull back and the mouth hiss open. *Astonishment,* Spock noted. *Perhaps other life forms recovering from sensory deprivation are disoriented, perhaps even mad. Shall I attempt to feign insanity? Negative. Without a speech common to us both the creature could not distinguish madness from coherent communication. Body language perhaps.*

Spock rose unassisted and stood with an impassive expression, dignified and aloof. The reptilian creatures looked at each other, their tongues twitchy and their hooded eyes watching him. Tails swung back and forth angrily.

The leader gestured, and a graceful Beta rose from the nestlike confines of one of the spherical structures and brought a silvery cage to the leader. He pointed, and the Beta took the cage to Spock. He could see within a small birdlike creature. When it fluttered its wings to maintain its balance on the perch, he could see there were four wings.

The Beta opened the cage door, and at once the bird attacked, its beak striking Spock's cheek and biting. There was a stinging sensation and Spock staggered, a dizziness momentarily unbalancing him. Then he was all right and the bird was lying on the floor, its wings beating frantically, then abruptly stopping.

All the reptilian-headed creatures shrank back. *My body chemistry killed the bird,* Spock thought. *Unfortunate creature, I apologize, but I cannot change my structure any more than you could overcome your genetic heritage and training.*

Spock was the attention of all eyes. He saw the short

swords in the hands of the Alphas. They began to close warily in on him.

■ ■ ■

Tom Collins flashed his light into the void of the great chamber and could barely make out the dark tiers opposite. "This must have been some place when it was working," he said. "The accomplishment here was tremendous."

McCoy snorted. "A monument to bureaucracy. I've always heard that bureaucrats tend to expand their little fiefdoms into kingdoms, but to cover an entire *world!* That's ridiculous!"

"I wonder what happened to the empire that this might have governed?" Bradley said.

"Maybe there wasn't any," Kirk said as they moved into a dark passage. "Maybe the snake of government just swallowed its tail."

"The governing *of* the people became the entire society?" asked McCoy.

"Perhaps. There's no sign of alien cultures here. No artifacts, museums, starships. Nothing to indicate outlying colonies. It's monolithic. The end product of bureaucracy."

"But why kidnap Mister Spock?" Bradley asked.

Kirk shrugged. "Trophy. Hostage. Mister Spock *was* the one different from the rest of us, so perhaps scientific curiosity. Those great creatures back there . . . *apparently* little more than semi-intelligent animals. I would have approached them differently, but—or it—gave us no choice."

"Sir," asked Bradley, "shouldn't we wait for the combat teams? I mean, those critters are *big*!"

"There may not be time. Spock might be in danger."

■ ■ ■

As the huge Alphas lumbered toward him, Spock acted. With blinding speed he jumped at the nearest of the gray-green creatures and kicked at his sword arm, sending the weapon spinning away toward a pavilion full of startled Betas.

Spinning, Spock spun on his feet, and his strong kick sent the startled Alpha tumbling backward. Out of the corner of his eye Spock saw the Beta leader lifting the rod-and-sphere. Spock leapt, rolled, and came up with a booted heel striking at the weapon, knocking it from the grasp of the Beta, who cowered back.

Spock rolled over and snatched up the rod and pointed it at the advanced Alphas, who instantly stopped. Spock felt no trigger, and a quick glance told him there was none on the half-meter rod. *But they don't know I can't operate it,* he thought, keeping it aimed at them.

"Now, gentlemen and ladies," Spock said, "shall we all just sit down." He gestured with the rod, and after several repeats they all got the idea and even the hulking Alphas sat on the floor.

"We shall now begin to communicate," the Vulcan said.

■ ■ ■

"Hurry," Kirk whispered. The corridors had become cleaner and they had passed more rooms showing signs of habitation. But no more of the big gray-green creatures.

Then they saw the great hatch. The two guards fell with a clatter as they were hit with stunning beams from the phasers. There was, to Kirk's mind, no time for niceties, not when Spock might be in danger.

They pulled open the hatch carefully. The warm and scented air struck them at once. Phasers in hand, the humans moved slowly and cautiously through the hatch opening.

"Greetings, Captain," Spock said.

"Spock, what in the name of sanity are you doing?" McCoy demanded.

Kirk smiled. "Yes, Mister Spock, just what are you up to?" Kirk looked around the huge room, at the gazebos and pavilions, at the platforms and exotic luxury—and at the two alien races seated in arcing rows before Spock.

"Endeavoring to conduct a class in interspecies communication, Captain. It would have helped had we thought to beam down a universal translator, but I am making do."

"Indeed you are," McCoy said wryly.

A platform had been upended and used as a blackboard, with figures drawn to indicate Alphas, Betas, and human/Vulcans, each with a symbol in Universal English. The phrases "world-state," "federation of planets," and "democratic government" had been written out.

"Sir, does this violate the Prime Directive?" asked Collins.

The rule of noninterference, General Order Number One, was a wise rule, allowing each culture to develop on its own, thus ensuring variety, strength, and versatility to the intelligent races. But there were many exceptions. One was when the vital interests of the Federation were threatened, but it also allowed for careful and judicious use of action to restore a balance. The natives of this nameless world were merely having the social structure of the civilized planets explained to them, and communication was to be established.

"No, Lieutenant, I don't believe it does. Go back the way we came, stop the combat teams, and get a universal translator beamed down here. And ask for a volunteer to stay here awhile to indoctrinate these people on the Federation."

Collins nodded and left at a trot. "Mister Spock, excuse me," Kirk said.

"Captain?"

"Spock, you were kidnapped and now we find you the mentor to two races. Would you care to explain?" The eyes of both Alphas and Betas turned curiously toward the captain, then back to Spock.

"Captain, I have been able to determine the past history of both these races to a certain extent. The larger of the two races are called Folonix; the smaller, the Granotoulomines. They are the indigenous races of this system, evolving on two planets. The Granotoulomines were apparently great organizers, but the Folonix were not. Gradually the one took over both planets. The planet and moons of the Folonix were used as raw material to create this structure, and the Folonix became a subject race without a home. They never developed stardrive, and this civilization fed on itself."

"Every civilization based on slavery has fallen, sooner or later," Kirk said.

"The added weight gradually deflected this world from its customary orbit, causing great damage, and death. The social structure was so rigid that once the systems started to break down, it went very quickly. Disease appeared, and these are the survivors."

"Decadent survivors," Bradley said.

"Not quite, Mister Bradley," Spock said.

"Explain," Kirk requested.

"They accepted the situation. Too few in number to rebuild their shattered inner empire, they accepted things as they are."

"Their fate," McCoy said.

"In a way," Spock replied. "They *are* natural bureaucrats. To them, 'fate' is the naturally achieved goal of completion. To them life had an order, a progression."

"But they had a slave race," protested Pat Bradley.

"The Folonix evolved on a planet farther from the sun, I would guess, and the colder, outer passages were more comfortable than the overheated quarters of the Granotoulomines. They each provided services to the other."

McCoy said, "Together they were waiting for the end."

"Again, not quite correct, Doctor McCoy. They awaited the completion of the cycle, the process of order. They have accepted our entrance into their lives as the transition to another level of progress. They are amazingly good students, eager to learn, adaptive and orderly."

McCoy groaned. "And bureaucratic."

"Perhaps, Doctor, but logical, too, if not imaginative. Any effort of importance requires discipline and order. They have it, both of them."

Bradley spoke up. "Mister Spock, they are so . . ." He

could not seem to find the words, but his tone told Spock much.

"Mister Bradley, to them *we* are ugly. You see, on one hand, a reptilianlike appearance, and in human cultures the reptile has always been a phobia. You see in he Folonix great hulking beasts out of some children's horror story, ogres in dark metal caves. But to both these races we are hairy, fragile, puny creatures with an incomprehensible desire to wear clothing in a stable environment."

Bradley appeared chastened, and Captain Kirk prepared everyone to return to the surface to be beamed aboard.

"Sir?" Bradley said. "May I volunteer to stay?" Kirk looked at him a moment.

"Certainly, Mister Bradley. We'll have supplies beamed down at once. Anything else you'd like?"

"Uh, could you fix it with Commander Scott? He, uh, he likes to keep his engine room crew together."

Kirk smiled. "I'll talk to Scotty. We'll pick you up in about two weeks, Standard Time." Kirk's expression softened still more. "At least we'll see if you're ready to come back aboard."

"Yes, sir, thank you, sir."

■ ■ ■

Trudging back up to a level where the transporter beam could get them, Kirk asked Spock a question. "What made you think the Folonix and the Granotoulomines were ready for a teacher?"

"Logic, Captain. They were highly xenophobic. They attempted to control or kill me at first sight. Yet they didn't. I was taken as a *specimen*, and they did not kill me when I was totally helpless. Therefore, curiosity was a stronger element than xenophobia. Their fear of anything strange was less than their desire to learn." Spock shrugged. "I merely accelerated that desire by obtaining the upper hand and changing the conditions of the relationship."

"You know, Spock, when you explain something it always sounds so logical."

"Does that surprise you?" Spock said, looking at his captain with raised brows.

"No, not after all these years, but what *does* surprise me—still—is that in the midst of combat, in the middle of a physical or psychic or even *telepathic* struggle, you can manage to think so *logically*."

Spock's eyebrows ascended higher. "Really, Captain, you should understand that logic is logic whether it is swift or slow. Given all the facts, certain conclusions are inevitable."

"When do we ever get *all* the facts, my friend?"

"Sadly true, Captain. Logic states that experience proves that we seldom if ever are in possession of all the facts. Therefore, it is logical to postulate theoretical conclusions based on insufficient evidence."

Kirk sighed. "How did I know that would be your response?"

"Logic, Captain," Spock said.

"Spock, are you smiling?"

"*Me*, Captain?"

"No, that wouldn't be logical, would it?" Kirk shrugged, then shot a glance at his First Officer. "Spock?"

"Looked at from a certain viewpoint, Captain, even humor is logical," Spock said.

Kirk stopped walking and looked at his taller companion. "You know, Mister Spock, you are a neverending source of amazement to me." Spock looked slightly surprised. Kirk pulled out his communicator. "*Enterprise*, this is Kirk. Do you read me?"

"*Enterprise* here, Captain," Uhura said.

"Prepare to beam us up. We have a deadline to meet."

"Yes, sir."

"Oh, and put it on the ship's bulletin: beginning after we leave Base IV, Mister Spock will be conducting classes in arriving at logical conclusions derived from insufficient data."

"Really, Captain," Spock protested.

"Yes, sir," Uhura responded. "May I be the first to sign up?"

"Of course, Uhura, and I'm second. Some of us need it more than others."

Spock's expression grew sedate again. "That's logical, Captain," he said.

Kirk gave him a sharp look, but already the transporter beam was scanning them. There was a sparkling, and the gray metal corridor was empty.

As Old
As
Forever

"**C**aptain Kirk, distress call on the emergency band!"
Uhura said sharply.

"Put it on the screen," Kirk said, swinging his command chair around.

The image was streaked and blurred, then cleared up somewhat as Uhura worked on it. "It's coming from Hippocrates Four, sir," Uhura reported. "Osler, an Earth-type planet with a single colony."

". . . *rak* . . . *sturm* . . ." The words were scratchy and blurred, but gradually Uhura strengthened and clarified the distant signal. "*Help . . . anyone . . . we're the only ones left . . . help . . . need help . . . Help . . . anyone . . .*"

"It's a recorded transmission, sir," Uhura reported. "The computer says the colony was established fourteen years ago as a medical research center."

"Mister Sulu, chart a course for Hippocrates Four." The Chief Helmsman gave a crisp response, and the U.S.S. *Enterprise* altered its star-spanning flight.

■ ■ ■

"No life forms inconsistent with previous indications," Mister Spock reported. "Some grazing animals to the southwest of the station, but only one energy reading at the colony itself."

"Very well," Kirk said, thumbing a switch. "Lieutenant Collins, prepare a landing party to investigate the emergency."

"Aye, sir," the security officer responded. "Any indication of danger?"

Kirk smiled. "Every new planet is dangerous, Lieutenant. Standard precautions."

"Will you be accompanying us, sir?"

Kirk caught Spock's look. "No. No, Lieutenant, not this time. Kirk out." The lithe captain smiled at his First Officer. "You don't like me leaving the ship, do you, Mister Spock?"

"It does seem unnecessary at times, Captain. But I am learning more of human nature all the time."

"Meaning?"

"Meaning that one of the reasons the human race rose up into the stars is the very urge that makes you want to leave the bridge and beam down: to see." Spock shrugged.

"Mister Spock," Kirk said with a smile as he stood, "you have talked me into it."

"Captain, I had no intention—"

"C'mon, Spock, go with me. Breathing some air that hasn't been recycled a hundred times will do you good."

Spock snapped off a control. "Very well, Admiral Kirk, of course."

"Mister Sulu, you have the conn," Kirk said.

■ ■ ■

The surface of Osler was mostly drab and frozen tundra, with a band of habitable land at the equator. The medical station was a cluster of domes, interlocked by connecting passages. A kind of blue moss grew in patches all over the dome cluster. There were no lights except that of Collins and his men as they emerged from the main dome.

"Oh, Captain Kirk," Collins said in surprise. He gestured around at the tundra. "Mister Chekov would like this."

"Mister Chekov was raised in Leningora, an archeological structure housing almost a million people," Kirk said. "He hates snow."

"Well, we got a youngster here who loves it," Collins said, gesturing to his men to bring forth the child. "She doesn't want to go."

Kirk saw Doctor McCoy bend down as he talked to a child of about seven. She was pale and beautiful, staring with blue eyes at the red-coated security men. Then her eyes focused on Kirk and he felt a jolt, as though someone had touched his brain with a mild electrical shock.

"Jim, this is Pandora," the medico said, smiling. "She's the only survivor." The doctor came over to his commander and spoke to him and Spock quietly. "Her parents and all the rest died four years ago. Four years, Jim. She's been all alone, *here*, for four years. Luckily they had some protein-processing machines that didn't break down."

"What happened to her parents?" Spock asked, his eyes thoughtfully focused on the pale child.

"I don't know. The bodies . . . well, they're in one

room. She doesn't go in there, she says. I'll do an analysis, see if it is something contagious." He hesitated. "Jim, I hate to say it, but we'd better keep everyone here awhile. I'll bring down Doctor Chapel and we'll work as fast as we can."

"Very well, Doctor," Kirk said. He pulled out his communicator and gave some orders.

■ ■ ■

The little girl sat quietly in the prefabricated dome the *Enterprise* had beamed down. She was watching a children's television show about blue dragons invading Earth and being fought off by Thunderman. Admiral Kirk entered the dome and looked at her, then walked over to Spock, who was intent on a portable mega-tricorder.

"Spock."

"Captain." He indicated a screen, and Kirk raised his eyebrows. "That indicates the metabolic rate of our survivor." At Kirk's continued questioning stare, the Vulcan explained. "The most efficient I have ever seen. She quite literally gets every particle of nourishment from her food."

"Her mother would like that."

"Her mother may have caused it. The records show her mother to be Doctor Marie McDowell and her father Doctor Philippe Metchnikoff. Her mother won the Nobel and her father the Salk Award. Extremely well known, Captain. Their specialty was biology."

"Is that why they came here, to this?" Kirk asked, gesturing around. "Some kind of isolated experiments?"

Spock nodded. "Pandora was born here. Four years

ago, something happened. An automatic signal was sent." He looked at the child. "But why did she survive?"

"Perhaps McCoy can get answers."

■ ■ ■

"Phenomenal," McCoy said eagerly. "Jim, look at this. Her metabolic pathways are the most unusual I've seen. Her metabolite synthesis is—"

"Doctor!"

"Her catalism is—"

"Doctor McCoy! Bones!"

McCoy grinned apologetically, the tundra wind whipping his brown hair. "I'm sorry, it's just that she's a wonder, Jim, a medical wonder. She can live on scraps of food, on moss, or even just water. Her cells rebuild themselves almost at once. She's fantastically healthy and she'll live—I'd stake my reputation on it—she'll live almost forever!"

They all looked toward the dome where the girl was, and Kirk's scalp crawled; she stood in the hatch, just looking at them. Kirk took McCoy's arm and pulled him away.

It was getting toward dark and it was colder now, but the child, dressed in a simple thin jump suit, seemed unaffected. "Bones, is she . . . is she dangerous to the ship?"

McCoy looked astonished. "Jim, she's a child! A perfectly normal child. Well, she has been alone here, and . . . well, Jim, she's unusual, true, but . . ." He shook his head. "I don't see how."

"What have you found on the research being done here?" the starship officer asked.

"It's truly marvelous, Jim. I'm having the notes and equipment boxed up. It will be a monument to all of them."

"Yes, but why did they die?"

McCoy sobered. "I, I don't know yet." He looked around. "How many new worlds have we been on, Jim? Not just us, but Starfleet? Thousands? Millions? And no two alike. It is nature's treasure chest out here. There hasn't been one place where humans didn't need some kind of help. Domes like this, antitoxins, phasers, harvesting machines, and a thousand other aids."

McCoy looked back at the girl, still staring at them solemnly. "But what her parents discovered will give us an edge, Jim. Our bodies will become *really* efficient! We may become immune to disease, to wounds, to—"

There was an explosion in one of the domes. Shards of the moss-covered hemisphere flew in every direction and flames shot up. As Kirk whirled to order in the security people, he caught a glimpse of Pandora. She didn't seem surprised or startled . . . or afraid.

■ ■ ■

"Everything's ruined," McCoy said. "Everything. Some kind of electromagnetic impulse blanked the tapes, the notes and equipment were destroyed." The medic's shoulders slumped. "One of the greatest discoveries in the history of mankind, lost."

Spock stood nearby, watching McCoy report to his captain. But he was also looking at Pandora quietly watch a television show of mile-high green ogres striding across a purple sea to threaten tiny, cute cartoon people.

"Well, then, Doctor, let's go aboard and take Pandora

back to Earth," Kirk said. "She'll get the finest care and—"

"No."

They all looked at Pandora, who was still watching the screen. "I don't want to go back. It's scary there."

"Pandora," smiled Kirk, going to her. "What you're watching is just entertainment. It's not like that at all."

"They lie, then?"

"No, it's not lying, it's just . . . imagination. Didn't you have shows like this?"

"No. And I'm staying."

"Pandora, you can't stay here, not alone."

"Why not? I have."

"But that was—"

"No, Captain Kirk." The child was firm, and Kirk smiled as he stood up.

"Lieutenant Collins," he said into his communicator. "Prepare to beam aboard. Mister Spock, Doctor, Pandora—"

The child jumped up and was out the door with blinding speed. Even Spock was unable to grab her. Kirk and the others ran into the night, but she was out of sight.

Spock's tricorder showed no life form energy readings. An hour's search among the humps and gullys of the tundra turned up nothing. Kirk ordered everyone back to the ship.

"I'll stay here in the dome," he said. "Maybe she'll come back. If only one person is here she may not be afraid."

Reluctantly the others left. Kirk sat down on a portable chair and stretched his legs. *It's been a long time since I was a child,* he thought, *and a long time since I had much to do with children.*

He thought of her, out in the deepening cold of the night. Bone-chilling cold. The cold of death.

■ ■ ■

"Huh?" Kirk came awake with a start. Pandora stood there, looking at him. "Oh. Hello, child. Pandora. Do you want to go now?"

"No."

"Pandora, you—" He reached out to touch her, and there was a spark between his fingers and her cheek. Kirk was slammed back, falling backwards in his chair.

"I told you I didn't want to go," she said. "I just came to tell you to leave."

"But it's lonely here," Kirk said, getting up slowly.

"It's always been lonely here, and since all of you have come, it's crowded."

Kirk thought of a few people on the surface of an Earth-sized planet. "No, it's just that you're unused to—"

It was like a scream in his mind.

All she did was reach out to him, to touch him. Like fire the feeling streaked to his brain, and he fell backwards into unconsciousness.

■ ■ ■

Kirk awoke in an ice cave. It glittered dully in the light from several spots along the rock peeking through the ice. Here moss grew, and the shallow yellow light came from hand-sized spots.

No, he realized, from hand-*shaped* spots. Child's hands. A child had touched the moss and it glowed.

He was cold, bone-cold. Even the built-in heat controls in his landing suit had been overloaded. His nose, hands, and feet felt numb. The ice was all around in great clumps and crystals. And he was alone.

Kirk got to his feet, his teeth chattering. Then he heard movement and turned to see Pandora come gracefully around a turn in the cave's icy wall. She looked pale and pretty, dressed in a thin blue jumpsuit with embroidered pink and red flowers.

"Pandora, what happened?"

"Oh, good, Captain, you're awake."

"How did I get here?"

"I brought you here," she shrugged. She handed him a packet of concentrated food. "I found this in the dome. It's too rich for me, but maybe you—"

"*Pandora*, you're a child, you couldn't have lugged me in here! Now who else is here?"

"No one." She looked at him, then put down the packet on a hump of ice. "Didn't Doctor McCoy tell you about me?"

"Yes, but—"

"I'm really very strong when I must be, you know. I just think about it and I get very, very strong. I learned it myself," she said proudly. "Mommy and Daddy didn't know I could. Course, I was only three then. They were trying to make me do something." She shrugged and sat down primly on another hump of ice. "They were always trying to make me do things I didn't want to."

"Pandora, they . . . they were your parents, they were trying to do what was good for you."

She shrugged and smoothed the legs of her jump suit. "Maybe. I dunno. I think I was more like an experiment to them. Maybe they weren't even my real parents."

Kirk sighed and squatted down near her. She watched him a little warily. "Lots of children think . . . well, they sometimes think their parents aren't their real parents because they don't get along with them at times. But—"

"I don't want to talk about that, Captain Kirk. I want you to tell me a story."

"Darling, I'll tell you all kinds of stories, but first we'll go up to the ship and—" It was then Kirk discovered he had neither phaser nor communicator. "Where are my things, Pandora? I want them returned."

"No. I hid them. They can't find you here. I found out about Mister Spock's tricorder and the sensors on the ship. That's why we're here. They can't read us here. And you can't get out. I iced up the entrance."

Kirk looked at her for a moment. "You want to kill me?"

"No. I want you to tell me stories."

"But I'll die here. I'll freeze. So will you."

Pandora laughed gaily, smiling for the first time. "Oh, you're funny! I can't freeze! Not ever. I can use the ice to get energy. I'm really very good at it, I found out. Vegetable matter is easier, but I can get energy from just about anything."

She smiled and motioned for him to sit on a hump of ice. "Really, Captain, you're very funny. I like to laugh. It's so strange, laughing, when you think of it."

"Pandora . . . dear . . . I'm the captain of a starship. They need me. I can't stay here telling you stories and—"

"Captain, I don't *care*. You came here and now I'm

going to have someone to play with. I thought about Mister Spock, but he's spooky. And Doctor McCoy, well, he wanted to take my blood, just like the others."

"The others?"

"Mommy and Daddy and the others. They were always taking my blood and reading me with things and all that. I finally told them to stop, and when they wouldn't I made them."

A chill went over Kirk; it had nothing to do with the surrounding ice. "You . . . made them . . . stop?"

She nodded. "Uh-huh. I don't want to talk about it. I was only three or four, you know. But they just wouldn't leave me alone. Now, tell me a story. About how the ice man flew to the sun. That's a good one."

"I don't know that one, Pandora." Kirk started to kneel next to her, to tell her of the importance of getting back. But the child shrank back and put her chubby little hand on his face.

Intense whiteness.

Pain. Spots. Blackness.

A faint red haze seemed to be over everything. He was falling, in slow motion, crashing back into the ice, breaking it, falling, sliding . . . pain . . . red . . . black . . .

■ ■ ■

"You've got to stop doing that," Kirk said with a moan. "I mean you no harm."

"You scared me." She pouted. "You shouldn't scare me. I don't like that. The cheebors scared me and I made them go away, too."

"Cheebors?" Kirk sat up groggily, testing his body for bruises and wounds.

"The grazers. They're very territorial, my father said. I can't go walking without them running at me."

"And you—?"

"I found one asleep and I touched him and he ran off and told the others, I guess, and they haven't been back."

"Pandora, I really must insist. Come back to the ship. Everyone will be worried."

"No, they won't. Not anymore. While you were resting I went up and checked. There were all kinds of people there, but they went away."

"Went away?"

"Very pretty really. They just sparkle and go away."

"Pandora, how long have I been down here?" Jim Kirk was suddenly very aware of a deep hunger and a bone-weary weakness.

"Oh, I don't know. Twelve turnings, I guess. They've gone, though. I knew they would because my Daddy said humans are very impatient."

"Humans? You're human, Pandora."

"Oh, I suppose so. Tell me about the elves. I like stories about elves and princesses."

"Pandora, twelve turnings is more than two standard *weeks*! I can't—"

"Yes, you can, Captain Kirk. Now stop complaining *and tell me a story!*"

Kirk rose to his full height and looked down on the child. "I've never threatened a child in my life, but I have responsibilities to my ship. You will take me out of here at once and we will go back to the *Enterprise* and this whole silly thing will be over!"

The little girl smiled up at him. "Oh, it's just like Mommy said some men get! It's really good, Captain

Kirk, really." She hugged herself with glee. "Go on, tell me how you will clap me in irons or make me walk the plank! I love it when people do that!"

"*Pandora!*" Kirk roared and shook his fists in frustration. There was a clink and tinkle of breaking ice somewhere off out of sight in the maze of frozen water.

The child clapped her hands in glee. "Oh, marvelous! Oh, great! More! More!"

Then Kirk made the mistake of grabbing her again.

■ ■ ■

It was as if he had grabbed a meteor. Color and light streaked around him, sound roared in his ears. His muscles, tensed and hard, seemed about to pull his body apart.

He *soared* in a volcano of sensation, as though his nervous system had been wired to a carnival. Kirk thought he screamed, but he wasn't certain.

Then it was over.

He lay limply, sprawled on the chilly, rough surface of the ice cave. The girl bent over him. "Are you all right? I'm sorry, I didn't mean to hurt you. Please, Captain, speak to me!"

Kirk stirred and started to sit up, then shrank back as she reached for him. "Oh, no, don't worry," she said. "But when you grabbed me . . . well, I just can't help it. Mommy said some people scream or jump, and I, well, I *react*."

"You certainly do," Kirk said. Everything seemed to hurt, and he moved stiffly.

"Let me help," she said and put her hands on each side of his neck before he could react.

It was as though honey flowed over his body. The pain, the fatigue, even the hunger just dissolved away. He heaved a great sigh of relief and sat up. "I feel marvelous," he said with a smile. "Never better. How do you do that?"

"I'm not sure," she said solemnly. "It has something to do with activating and helping your natural immune system. I mean, when you walk you don't really tell your feet to move individually, do you? You just *walk*; same with this."

"McCoy will be fascinated," Kirk said, standing up. "Now, let's just get out of here and everything will be—"

"Captain, haven't you been listening? I don't want to go. Being with people is . . . well, all of you move in clouds of bacteria, in auras of electrochemical energy. It is very hard for me to cope with that."

"But—"

"Captain, it's like . . . like someone is playing really *loud* music right next to you, do you understand? You can't think, do anything. I just want to be left here. But you can entertain me. One or two people I can take. If I get too many around me, I . . ." She looked sad, and suddenly she was crying.

Kirk hesitated to put his arms around her, but he did. There was no reaction, and for a long time she just sobbed against him. *Alone since she was three,* he thought. *Four years old on a hostile, alien planet. And she lived, she coped, she survived. She talks like an adult, but she has the body and the development of a child.*

"Is that what happened to . . . to the research staff?" he asked, and she nodded against him, sniffing at her tears.

After a moment she pulled back and turned away. "I

couldn't help it. I was just a baby. I barely remember. They . . . they were always after me. Taking blood—I *hate* that—and testing, testing. I got sick and . . . I had a fever . . . I kind of remember that. I . . . I struck back."

She looked up at Kirk. "I couldn't help it, Captain. You know when they hit your knee and your foot goes up? It was like that. I sort of sent out . . . I don't know, spores, I guess. I called them wizards then. Little wizards no one could see."

She fell silent, her eyes staring into the past. Kirk stroked her shoulders, his heart going out to the child's pain. "They . . . they made me that way, you know. My immune system is *very* good. My metabolism can provide the energy. I . . . I've read about it since. Their notes, and the books." Pandora moved off a few feet and spoke thoughtfully.

"A baby cries, throws a tantrum . . . and that's what I did, Captain Kirk. Only what I did killed them all. I didn't know they weren't like me, that they couldn't stand against my wizards. That's why I must never go to where people are. Not ever. I couldn't trust myself not to . . . not to . . ." She started crying again and trotted to him to hold her.

■ ■ ■

"*Enterprise,* this is Kirk."

"Captain!" Montgomery Scott said in surprise and delight. He thumbed a transmitter control on the captain's control chair. "Where are you, sir? We've been—"

"Later, Scotty. Beam in on these coordinates and bring the two of us aboard."

"Aye, sir!" Scott gave orders to the transporter room

crew and then signaled to Spock. "Mister Spock, forgive me for waking you up, I know you've only had an hour's sleep after three days awake, sir, but—"

"What is it, Mister Scott?" Spock said evenly from his cabin.

"The captain, sir, he's alive!"

"Good, Mister Scott. I shall come to the bridge at once."

"Good? That's all you can say, Mister Spock? *Good*? He's been missing for *two weeks*, Mister Spock!"

"I'm well aware of that, Mister Scott. The very fact that I kept the *Enterprise* in orbit here while we broadened the search is proof of that."

"Aye, Mister Spock," Scott said moodily. He broke the transmission, and to no one at all in the control room he said, "Sometimes I don't understand Vulcans at all."

There was more than one silent nod around the room.

■ ■ ■

McCoy looked up from his scope and grinned at Pandora. "You're as healthy as a horse," he said.

"Healthier." She smiled back.

McCoy turned to Captain Kirk. "Now you, Jim."

Kirk smiled. "I'm as healthy as a horse, too."

"I'll be the judge of that," the doctor grumbled. Kirk shrugged, winked at Pandora, and subjected himself to McCoy's inspection.

The medical officer ended by shaking his head. "You're right. There is nothing wrong with you. *Nothing* wrong. And that alone is kind of scary. Even some of your old scar tissue has disappeared."

Kirk put his arm around Pandora. "I made her a deal,

Bones. You don't take blood, you keep the probes and sensors to a *minimum*—and *she* decides what the minimum is—"

"But, Jim, she's—"

"Not anymore she isn't. She is no longer a specimen. She is a seven-year-old girl. A special seven-year-old, but just a seven-year-old girl."

"Jim, this is an opportunity—"

"Bones."

"The notes were lost, the tapes blanked. We won't know what her parents and the others were doing unless—"

"Bones, calm down. She'll cooperate. She just doesn't want to be a *subject* anymore, you understand?"

McCoy looked at Pandora's big dark eyes and sighed. "A week at Memory Alpha? At Luna Lab? Johns Hopkins?" Pandora shook her head firmly. "You mean, all I get is . . . is what I've got?"

Kirk nodded. "One blood sample, one *brief* examination. And then I put my career on the line and lie."

"Lie?" McCoy looked startled.

"Well, let's say I just don't tell of *everything* that happened on Osler. Pandora was the only survivor of a mysterious accident and illness. I was lost for two weeks and have little memory of it. And Pandora saved my life by keeping me awake."

McCoy sighed. "And my research?"

"Based on what you put together from what scraps you could find—which is true—and Pandora can live a normal life."

"No, Jim," McCoy said softly, looking at the little girl. "She will never live a *normal* life. But it will be a very long life. A *very* long life. Her cells don't age, they don't build up the toxins which destroy us all in the end. She, she could live . . . forever."

Pandora blinked. Her chin quivered just twice. "You mean, I . . . I would get to be as old as you are, Doctor?"

Kirk burst out laughing, and after a moment of indignation, so did McCoy. "Yes, my dear, this old. And maybe a wee bit older."

Spock entered the medical facility and looked at the three laughing, for Pandora had joined in with her tinkling laugh.

"May I ask the reason for this hilarity?" the Vulcan said.

"Top secret, Spock," McCoy said with a smile.

Spock's eyebrows went up. "You mean you are classifying Pandora's fascinating immune system as secret, Doctor?" McCoy stopped laughing. "It was the only logical conclusion, Doctor McCoy. A biological research team of the highest quality on a remote and hostile planet. They are mysteriously killed and a three-year-old child survives alone for four years."

Spock looked directly at the girl. "Fascinating," he said. "I realized you must have hidden Captain Kirk away in such a way as to fool our sensors. There was no indication of excavations into bedrock, so therefore you had reduced his—and your—vital signs to a minimum. That only could be done by an astonishing control of your metabolic system. It was therefore only a matter of time before you revived the captain and he had an opportunity to talk to you."

Kirk and McCoy stared at the Vulcan, but Pandora went to him and took his hand. Spock looked faintly surprised. "Oh, you feel funny," she said, and giggled. "You feel kind of . . . bubbly."

McCoy's eyebrows went up. "*Bubbly?*"

"C'mon, Mister Vulcan," Pandora said. "I bet you could tell me some marvelous stories."

Spock did not say a word as the little girl led him away.

McCoy looked at Kirk. " 'Bubbly'? 'Stories'? 'Mister Vulcan'? Jim, what—"

"Don't ask, Bones," Kirk said. "And remember: no blood samples."

■ ■ ■

In his cabin, Spock was speaking softly, and Pandora's large eyes were upon him intently. "Once upon a time, there was a beautiful princess who lived in a castle on a planet far, far away."

"What was her name?" the girl asked.

"Princess Pandora was her name," Spock replied.

"Oh, good," Pandora said. "Go on, please."

"Princess Pandora lived in a castle that had seven towers and . . ."

■ ■ ■

"Mister Sulu, Warp One for Memory Alpha, the information planetoid."

"Aye, aye, sir."

The stars began to sail majestically past, then blur and streak as they went into hyperdrive.

■ ■ ■

"And the handsome prince tugged at the huge dilithium crystal until the magic sword came out with a roar . . ."